He mustn't guess her secrets.

Alanna looked up, suddenly facing the amorous threat of those deep blue eyes. She knew she was violently attracted to Jeremy Masters. It was a kindling of an inner fire, a fire she hadn't known existed. And she had thought she'd loved Tim. . . It had never felt like this with Tim. Never this fire, these tendrils of desire.

Dear Reader

Can you put the past behind you? Jenny Ashe poses this question in THE CALL OF LOVE, while Sarah Franklin looks at obsessive behaviour in THE WESSEX SUMMER. No claims for a cure, but sometimes help can be found. In WAITING GAME, Laura MacDonald explores the passage from infatuation to love, in a touching story, while Judith Worthy gives us a heroine who married the wrong brother—the right one is *very* right. . . Australian Cam Walters is every woman's dream!

See you next month!

The Editor

Lancashire-born, **Jenny Ashe** read English at Birmingham, returned home with a BA and rheumatoid arthritis. Married in Scotland to a Malaysian-born junior surgeon, she returned to Liverpool with three Scottish children when her husband became a GP in 1966. She has written non-stop since then—articles, short stories, radio talks, and novels. She considers the medical environment compassionate, fascinating and completely rewarding.

Recent titles by the same author:

TENDER MAGIC
FROM SHADOW TO SUNLIGHT

THE CALL OF LOVE

BY

JENNY ASHE

MILLS & BOON LIMITED
ETON HOUSE   18–24 PARADISE ROAD
RICHMOND   SURREY   TW9 1SR

First published in Great Britain 1992
by Mills & Boon Limited

© Jenny Ashe 1992

Australian copyright 1992

ISBN 0 263 13259 5

Set in 10 on 11 pt Linotron Times
15-9205-57306

Typeset in Great Britain by Centracet, Cambridge
Made and printed in Great Britain

CHAPTER ONE

'GOOD morning, Sister Keith. It's a pleasure to meet you at last—and kind of you to step in like this at such short notice.' Jeremy Masters was a man who was very easy to like. Apart from the infectious smile, hidden at the moment by his surgical mask, his deep blue eyes twinkled attractively as he strolled into theatre pressing his gloves more firmly by meshing his fingers together. He was well known as the calmest and most agreeably tempered surgeon in the entire hospital, and this cheerful greeting seemed to prove it.

So why was Alanna Keith decidedly on guard this morning? Because, quite simply, Mr Masters was a ladykiller. It was only to be expected, given his looks, his athletic figure and his reputation as a gifted surgeon, achieving senior registrar grade at the age of twenty-eight. He had no trouble charming the feminine sex into his arms, and it was also well known that he had taken every advantage of his charisma to escort most of the available nurses in Faireholme Hospital, while still succeeding in remaining totally uncommitted to any of them. For reasons of her own, Alanna had no intention of allowing him to add her to his list of conquests, and had made a point of avoiding him—until today, when his regular theatre sister had been struck down with viral pneumonia. Alanna was the only replacement free. In her most non-committal tone, she said briskly, 'No problem. I'd be transferring here to Orthopaedics next month anyway.'

Jeremy's voice purred, and his interested glance above the mask was fairly predictable, given Alanna's

slim blonde prettiness and her intelligent dark-fringed
eyes. 'Lucky us! So we'll be working together. Could
be the start of an interesting partnership.'

Alanna said quietly, 'I'm quite ready to start, Mr
Masters. The first operation, I mean.' She felt her
cheeks grow warm, and was glad of the protection of
her mask.

His tone was amused. 'Jeremy, please—it's first
names here, you know. I prefer my colleagues to think
of us all as a group of friends when we work together—
don't I, Steve?' He directed his question at his consultant anaesthetist, Stephen Fitzwalter, who was grey-
haired and dignified, and the last person Alanna would
have dared to call by his first name. Jeremy went on,
as Dr Fitzwalter turned to meet the trolley bearing
their first patient of the morning, 'What's *your* first
name, Sister?'

As it was obvious that the young surgeon had no
intention of going ahead with his work until she
answered him, she briefly gave her name, and turned
away to the instrument tray, straightening shiny retractors and scalpels that were already perfectly aligned
and ready for use. With that he appeared satisfied, and
with a final glance at her downcast eyes he gave the go-
ahead for the Pentothal to be injected by the taciturn
Dr Fitzwalter. The conversation became technical.
'This is an injury to the radius and ulna. Poor chap was
brought in last night, and needed a transfusion before
we could operate. Rock-climbing can be a dangerous
hobby. Remember that, and stick to—what is it you
do in your spare time, Alanna?'

'I'm a member of the community leisure centre.' Her
reply was terse, as Jeremy Masters slit the fascia over
the crushed wrist bones and deftly lifted broken pieces
of the ulnar head out of his way with forceps. Alanna
started suction at his signalled request, giving him a

better view of the battlefield of twisted sinews and bloodstained slivers of bone that had once been a healthy wrist.

'God!' For a moment even Jeremy Masters' calm was shaken. 'How did this get in such a mess? I'm not sure where to start.' But he started, methodically probing further back, searching for the point at which the bone started looking normal. 'It must have been some fall.'

The houseman said, 'I think his friend said that, after the fall, a lump of rock fell on his arm.'

Jeremy Masters took a deep breath, and exhaled with a whistle. 'Looks as though half of Helvellyn fell on his arm! Well, he came to the right place. We'll soon sort him out.' Confident words, but Alanna stole a sidelong glance at him, and saw sweat already breaking out on the handsome tanned forehead. He was under pressure, but had no intention of showing it. Calmly she waited until he raised his head, then reached out gently and wiped the sweat away before it dripped into his eyes and ruined his view. He paused for a moment. 'Thank you, Alanna.' And his voice was gentle too, as though it responded to the feather-like softness of her touch. He went on, 'This patient works as a climbing instructor. Unless we can make some sense of this jigsaw, he'll be out of a job.'

For a long time there was silence, except for the artificial breathing of the patient with the help of the anaesthetist, and the quieter but still laboured breaths of the surgeon and his houseman. All eyes were on the arm, stripped to its very skeleton, as a skilled and talented surgeon tried his best not to allow the injury to beat him. 'He's going to be all right—I know he is.' But the entire team knew that Jeremy's whispered words were a prayer rather than a certainty, in spite of his reputation for almost brash self-confidence.

'Where's the styloid? For heaven's sake the man must have had a styloid. Don't tell me those splinters are all that's left!' Jeremy muttered to himself, as he probed again, beckoned Alanna for a swab, and probed further into the wrist bones. 'Maybe I was wrong, folks.' His voice became jauntier, but Alanna still mopped the sweat from his brow without being asked. 'Maybe Helvellyn mountain has beaten me this time.'

'How much bone can we save, sir?' The houseman clearly thought it was hopeless.

'It's all here, lad. And don't call me sir!' He could raise a smile among the team even at such a crucial point in the operation. 'It's just going to take a whole lot more time than we planned for. These tiny splinters and the torn tendon didn't show clearly on the X-ray.'

As Alanna watched, handed the correct instruments when asked, and swabbed continually, she found her grudging admiration for Jeremy Masters the surgeon growing by the minute. He did live up to his reputation. He cared, and he was good. He wanted to do the best possible job, and that meant being slow and methodical. The morning slipped by, and Jeremy Masters was still piecing slice after slice of bone alongside each other, laying them painstakingly in place, until at last the shattered arm became recognisable as a human limb, under its covering of iodine-tinted skin, stitched up carefully, and immobilised until it could be encased in plaster.

Jeremy stood upright slowly, straightening his back and stretching his arms out wide as the patient was wheeled to the plaster-room. The others relaxed for a moment, and the houseman congratulated him. Jeremy said, 'I've only started the job. We all know that, if he doesn't have decent skilled nursing and superb physio-therapy, that repair doesn't stand a chance.' He looked out into the ante-room. 'Well, where's number two?

We're running late out there, you idlers! Wheel 'em in. Let's get this list rolling!'

It was a much more thoughtful Alanna Keith who stripped off her hospital gown later and dressed in her neat blue uniform. Not that she considered herself susceptible, but working for Jeremy Masters was quite an experience, and she found herself looking forward to the next operating session in two days' time. The regular sister wouldn't be well enough by then, and Alanna found herself smiling at the thought of watching Jeremy at work. There was a grace and artistry about his operating that combined with his dedication was a pleasure to be part of. And there was an attractive modesty about the way he had included himself only as part of a team, giving proper credit to the physios and nurses.

She paused at the door of the orthopaedic ward. Jeremy was just coming out, still in his theatre green, with the houseman and registrar close behind him. He stopped when he saw Alanna. 'Ah, here's the girl who made it all possible. Like to have a word with our brave mountaineer, Alanna?' He turned to the other doctors. 'You go on, fellers. I'll be along in a second. I'd like Alanna to meet Tim. I think he'd like to say thank you to her now that he's come round.'

The registrar gave Alanna a knowing look, and gestured the houseman to follow him. They too had a good working knowledge of how Jeremy operated with women, and they clearly knew when they weren't needed. Jeremy was left facing an uncertain Alanna, who knew when she was being manipulated, but some-how was left breathless and amenable by this fast-talking senior registrar with the twinkle. He said, 'The chief's pretty pleased with the way we handled Tim Howarth this morning.'

Alanna felt as though she had been thumped in the solar plexus. 'Howarth? The patient this morning was Tim Howarth?'

'Yes—do you know him?'

Know him? She had been engaged to Tim Howarth for two years, a long time ago when she was young and impressionable. Jeremy was waiting for an answer, with a quizzical lift of an eyebrow. 'He—used to coach at the sports centre. . . I thought he was working in the south somewhere. I had no idea that he——' She didn't go on. It must be plain to the perceptive surgeon that his theatre sister was waffling, and that meant there was more in the relationship than she was admitting. Alanna said shortly, 'Will he be all right?'

'I hope so, Alanna.' He was looking into her face, and she avoided his eyes, because they were the sort of keen intelligent eyes that bored right into one's secrets. 'He's in the side room. I'll come with you.'

'It's all right——' But she stopped, knowing that if Jeremy Masters wanted to come with her, he would go right ahead and come. He was the last person she wanted to witness her first meeting with Tim after their fiery and acrimonious parting. But there was nothing she could do, except pray she could maintain her coolness and self-control.

Her heart was thumping as she approached the still figure in the white bed, his right arm held up in a sling above his head beside the bed, and a drip in his other arm taped down with plaster. The bearded face seemed peaceful enough, but at her approach he opened his eyes and winced as he shifted position slightly. 'Yes, Sister?' The familiar voice from her past made her draw in her breath, and Tim looked at her more closely. 'My God—Alanna!'

'Try not to move, Tim.' She found herself reaching

for his good hand and holding it. 'You've had a bad fall.'

He tried to smile. 'I should have fallen on my head, eh? Then there'd be no damage?'

'You'll be all right, don't worry. I was at the operation. It went well.'

'So your good-looking young surgeon told me,' said Tim.

Alanna opened her eyes wide. How could he speak of Jeremy like that when he was right there? But when she turned, she realised that Jeremy had not followed her into the room after all. That was tactful of him, and she was grateful. She looked back at Tim. 'I had no idea you were working in the Lake District,' she told him.

'Why should you? We'd well and truly split up—I still have the ring to prove it.'

She said, slowly and deliberately, as she tried to marshal her thoughts and emotions, 'We can still behave like adults.'

He sighed, then winced again, as the physical after-effects of the operation reminded him it was wiser to keep still. 'I hope so, Ali.' He paused, then said casually, 'Your Mr Masters is a winner with the girls, though—so the nurses tell me.' He looked away as he said, 'But you were always the cool one, weren't you?' His voice dropped. 'I might even say cold——' but she saw him, even in his half-anaesthetised state, regret saying that. 'Maybe seeing me like this might start up your sympathy for me?'

Alanna said simply, trying to stop past bitterness coming between them just now, 'In this state, Tim, no one could deny you sympathy. You've had a rough deal, and I know your job's in question now—but I want you to know——'

'My job? Did they say that?'

She looked into his familiar face, the deep-set eyes permanently crinkled against the elements, it seemed, the lock of red hair falling over his forehead, that once she had admired as a starstruck teenager gazing at a master of all sports and martial arts. Protect all the weak, he had proclaimed. Teach all women that they have the capacity to learn how to protect themselves. 'Tim, I shouldn't have said that. Mr Masters thinks you'll be as good as new. Only—it'll take a lot of self-discipline. He's done what he calls the easy bit. Now it's up to you and your nurses—and the occupational therapists.'

Tim closed his eyes, the effects of the anaesthetic still affecting him. But his voice was firm as he said, 'Then there's no problem. I can handle it. I hope they keep the job open, though—I'll do my damnedest to get back to work.'

'I'm glad, Tim.' Alanna looked down with pity, but the childish love that was born of admiration and infatuation for an idol was dead. If only she had been less open about her hero-worship. It had hurt them both deeply. Alanna breathed in, reminding herself that hero-worship could hardly ever turn into true and equal love. Now she pitied Tim, admired him for his self-control, and his ability to cope with his injury without becoming too sorry for himself.

She watched him for a while. At first she knew he was awake, and hoping for her to say something more. But soon the anaesthetic after-effects sent him to sleep again, and Alanna turned and walked quietly towards the door. Her decision to break their engagement had been right. Tim was a great guy in his own way, but not the one for her. He had been a hero to her when she was little more than an idealistic teenager, before he'd proved that there was a dark side to his nature. . . But now, the sort of hero for Alanna had to be more than just muscles and bravado. He had to be someone almost like—like Jeremy Masters, maybe, with the manual skill and the mental courage to tackle and put together again the human body with all its accidents and infirmities. . .

Halfway along the corridor, she was aware that someone was walking behind her. Turning, she saw Jeremy, changed into his trousers and shirt now, smiling at her with a confident and sure arrogance. But his tone was caring. 'You found your friend in good spirits?'

What could she say? 'He seems to have accepted his condition,' she told him.

'You think he has the will to pull through?'

'I know he has.'

'You must have known him well.'

She was determined to give nothing away. 'Yes,' she said briefly.

'A member of the local sports club?'

'Yes.'

'I wonder why he left coaching badminton and judo to take risks on the Lakeland mountains?'

Alanna looked up, suddenly facing the amorous threat of those deep blue eyes. He mustn't guess her secrets. She knew she was suddenly violently attracted to Jeremy Masters. It was a kindling of an inner fire, a fire she hadn't known existed, and she stumbled over her reply, fearing that his personality would overwhelm her. And she had thought she loved Tim. . . It had never felt like this with Tim. Never this fire, these tendrils of desire. She managed to keep her voice reasonably calm. 'Tim had more to give, you see. He needed a challenge.'

'And you, Alanna? Aren't you the same type? Needing a challenge? Surely you aren't fully stretched

by an evening of badminton and a cup of cocoa or
carrot juice at the leisure club?'

She wasn't ready for his question. She thought she
had sized up Jeremy Masters from a distance, over the
few months he had been at Faireholme, and although
she had hoped to escape his attention, she had prepared her answers, just in case he ever noticed her.
But she wasn't used to such a searchingly personal
question—nor to that apparently sincere blue gaze.
Her voice was low. 'I'm not looking for anything. I'm
just me. I'm happy in what I'm doing, and I don't want
to change anything.'

Jeremy put his hand on her shoulder, forcing her to
stop walking. The touch caused an imperceptible
shiver. She was apprehensive—yet didn't want him to
take his hand away. The inner fire flickered again. The
corridor was empty, shadowy, and his words seemed to
echo into her innermost secret being. He said quietly,
'Allow me to disagree, Alanna. I've seen something in
your eyes that speaks to me. I don't mean to offend
you—in fact, I'm saying no more just now. But I want
you to remember that when I first saw you, I read a
hunger in those pretty eyes above that mask—a hunger
for something that maybe you don't even realise you
want.' He smiled, a casual, dismissive smile. 'Don't
forget I was the first to see it, Alanna!' And he
squeezed her shoulder gently, before turning and striding quickly away.

She stood for a moment, until the door stopped
swinging where Jeremy Masters had gone out like a
miniature whirlwind. I'm not a beginner, she told
herself firmly. The Tim Howarth affair had taught her
not to believe those first girlish feelings of sexual
attraction. Yet this was different—and she wound her
fingers together, appalled at her own fear of the total
attention of someone as attractive as Jeremy. She

mustn't react, but sit it out, stay calm, and wait for him to turn his attentions to someone a little more yielding and willing and available. The Jeremys of this world could pick and choose their conquests. She lifted her chin and straightened her shoulders. The Alannas of this world just didn't give in to such obvious and seasoned campaigners. He would find out, soon enough. Yet Tim's words echoed in her memory— 'You're the cool one.' Frigid, did he mean? Memories long forgotten, of their last few bitter arguments, of his physical hunger, began to surface, and her step quickened along the corridor until she was almost running.

'How did it go, Alanna?' It was Sue Long from AED, Alanna's best friend and room-mate. 'Isn't he just the cutest little surgeon in the world? And how about those twinkling eyes?'

They were making their way towards the canteen, later, and Alanna had taken a grip on her emotions. She fell into step alongside her friend, and decided flippancy was the best way of hiding her inner turbulence. 'It was fantastic,' she smiled. 'Just fantastic!'

Sue's eyes lit up. 'Wow—he was that sexy, then?'

'He was that good a surgeon,' said Alanna firmly. 'He knows his job. He'll be a consultant in a year, I'm sure of it. And that's all, Sue.'

Sue looked hard at her. 'He didn't make a pass? He's unattached at the moment, you know. Gave Emma Forbes the elbow, I hear. I was sure he'd notice those big golden eyes of yours. Are you sure he didn't tell you you have nice eyes?'

Alanna suddenly didn't want to go into details. She said with some hesitation, 'The first patient—he was Tim Howarth, Sue. You remember? I told you I was engaged when I was seventeen to a judo instructor? It was Tim Howarth. He's a mountain guide now—and his right arm was terribly mangled in a rock fall.'

'I'm sorry, Al. Was it very bad?'

'Jeremy did a marvellous job. But it was totally crushed. It'll be a miracle if Tim gets full use of that arm again.'

Sue said, 'I shouldn't have been so nosy. I'm sorry again.'

'Don't be,' Alanna smiled. 'And you were quite right, of course—Jeremy is quite a dish. But I think I can safely say it's a dish I'm allergic to. I don't like men who are aware of their charm. Handsome or not— you can have him, Sue! I want no closer encounters with Jeremy Masters than I've had today.'

Sue looked at her, as they pushed open the door to the cafeteria. She grinned. 'I wonder how long it will take him to get to you! When I first saw him, I thought you'd suit each other so well. You both have that wicked little twinkle in your eyes! All right, Al, he's played the field a bit. But destiny has to get him in the end. Someone has to be his destiny! Don't forget that!'

Alanna took a deep breath. 'At the moment, Sue, all I want is a bite to eat, and a nice straightforward game of badminton. Coming?'

Her friend pointed through the window. 'Look, Al— sunshine. Spring is here! You don't want to spend a nice May evening inside a stuffy sports centre, do you?'

From the corner of her eye Alanna spotted Jeremy Masters sitting at a table talking earnestly with his consultant, the famous and very rich orthopaedic genius, Mr Francis Bates. No doubt he was giving a blow-by-blow account of his surgical prowess that morning. Through the dining-room window the gentle glow of spring tinted the sky with translucent pink as the sun prepared to set behind the mellow grey stone of the hospital buildings. Alanna suddenly didn't want another enounter with Jeremy Masters that day. 'Shall

we walk along to the Robin's Nest and eat there?' she
said. 'I think I feel like a stroll.'

Sue had noticed Jeremy Masters too, and to her
credit she said nothing. 'Good. We both need some
fresh air. And it's Friday—there may be a disco later.'

'I am in the badminton team. . .' But Alanna gave
in, and the two girls walked the mile along the sub-
urban road, enjoying the cherry blossom in the gardens, and the loud chirruping of the amorous
blackbirds in the hedges. 'The team can manage without me for one night.' She firmly squashed her guilt
feelings. Badminton would make her think of Tim.
And thinking of Tim would make her think of
Jeremy. . .

But in the morning their telephone shrilled before
either girl was up. 'It'll be for you,' said Sue diving
under her duvet. Alanna was just as tired, after dancing
until late, but she reached out and took the phone.
'Hello?'

It was the badminton team coach. 'What happened
to you yesterday, Al? I only had three players at first.'

The guilt feelings came back, and Alanna was
ashamed of her own weakness, letting a cocky registrar
affect her like that. 'I'm sorry, Fred—I didn't feel up
to it. Long day in the operating theatre.'

'That's funny, because we had one of your surgeons
wanting to join us last night. Name of Masters. Said
he'd spent a long day in the operating theatre too—
and felt that a game of badminton was just the thing to
loosen him up! Good job he showed!'

There was a pause. Alanna said, when she had got
over the shock, 'I'll be there on Wednesday, coach—
promise!' She put the phone down, and sat up against
the pillow very thoughtfully.

'What's the matter?' queried Sue.

'Nothing. . .' Alanna didn't want to believe that

Jeremy had joined the club simply to get her interest. But that was surely the way it looked, with him turning up the very day that he had found out what Alanna did in her spare time.

She was down for theatre the following Monday. It was essential to show Jeremy that she neither knew or cared about his application to join the leisure club. As she pulled on her theatre clothes, she didn't look up as she heard the low murmur of male voices. She was a nurse, only here to do a job.

'Morning, Sister Keith.'

And Alanna knew she felt a tiny twinge of disappointment to see Francis Bates coming to take the morning list instead of Jeremy. 'Oh, good morning, Mr Bates.'

It was the houseman who asked where Jeremy was. Francis Bates replied cheerfully, 'Had to see a man about a dog, old chap. You know Masters, always got fingers in various pies around the town. But I owe him a session, so I don't mind doing today.' He chuckled. 'I don't ask about his private life—a bit lurid for me, don't you know! Now, who have we got on our list this morning?' As he checked through the list Alanna held for him, he went on, 'I hear you did a damn good job last week. Masters was impressed. But then, as he mentioned, with eyes like yours, Sister, I'm not really surprised.' And he winked, and beckoned for the first patient to be brought in.

Alanna went to visit Tim that afternoon, taking him apples and oranges. 'You'll have to peel them for me, Al,' he pleaded. His arm was still hauled up above his head, the ends of the fingers swollen. He said, 'It's the waiting that's frustrating—not knowing if the op's going to be a success. Apparently we won't know for up to six weeks.'

'You always were impatient when you had to keep still, Tim.'

A note of tension crept into his voice—a touch of thinly veiled sarcasm, perhaps? 'I know—a proper little action man—OK, maybe it will teach me patience. I probably needed it. Or so some people used to tell me.'

She looked at him sadly. Yes, it had been his temper that had started to drive her away; his temper and his inability to understand when she wanted him to leave her alone. . . The memories struggled back to the surface—his grasping hands, his panting breath, terrifying her because he was so strong. She paused, and didn't look into his face. 'I'm sure you'll be all right,' she told him. 'You're young and fit.'

'You'll come and see me again, Al?'

'Of course.' But she didn't like the little-boy look he was putting on. She hoped he wasn't making plans and beginning to want her back.

'Why hasn't young Lochinvar come to see me again? I thought he considered my arm a bit of a challenge.'

'I don't know, Tim. I think he's away for a day or two.' But as she walked along the corridor, she noticed through the front window that Jeremy Masters was standing there beside his red Porsche, hands in pockets, talking with animation to a very pretty brunette. So Emma Forbes was back. As Alanna watched, Emma seemed to give in and agree to something Jeremy had said. He opened the car door and helped her into the passenger seat. Alanna was standing, staring, when Jeremy suddenly looked up at the window, straight into her startled face, before walking round the car, smiling broadly to himself.

CHAPTER TWO

ALANNA was sitting in the garden of the Robin's Nest, enjoying the smooth balmy air of a perfect spring evening. She couldn't get the image of Jeremy Masters out of her subconscious. After the few words they had exchanged in the corridor after the operation on Tim, he had said very little directly to her. Yet in the succeeding weeks he had joined the leisure club—and he had made sure that Alanna was watching when he invited Emma into his Porsche. It was trivial, she told herself, yet she found herself lying awake at night, recalling every word he had ever said to her, every tiny compliment and every teasing glance.

Sue came out with two glasses of shandy and put them down on the wooden table. 'What a heavenly evening, Al. What shall we do tonight?'

'I'm whacked, Sue. An early night for me.'

'Rubbish—you never go to bed early! You're having me on. You must have a secret date you don't want to tell me about.'

Alanna looked into her friend's wide blue eyes. 'You know me better than that, Sue.'

'I know we've always shared all our secrets—so far. But you look different lately. Sort of wistful. . .you aren't worrying about Tim Howarth, are you? He's doing very well. They think he's going to be all right.'

Wistful. It reminded her of Jeremy's words. Don't forget I was the first to notice, he had said. Alanna said briskly, 'I'm not the wistful type, and you jolly well know it. I'm the most uncomplicated person in the whole of Faireholme.'

'So you aren't worried about Tim?'

Not worried about his medical problem. But when he was well again? She said firmly, 'No, not a bit. I was at the operation, remember? I know that Jeremy did everything humanly possible to make sure Tim's arm gets to being as good as new.'

'And you aren't even a tiny bit worried that Tim might want to start up with you again?'

Alanna shook her head, blushing as her friend read her thoughts. 'No. It's over. I'm not worried about anything at all, Sue—honest!'

'Then let's go to the fair! Did you know they're setting it up at Bishop's Corner? Shall we let our hair down and go on the roundabouts? And the Big Dipper? It's ages since the fair came to town.'

'I'd love it,' smiled Alanna. Faireholme was a quiet little town, and it would make a lively change to do something quite different and light-hearted. 'How much money can we scrape together between us?'

They counted their coins, putting aside enough for the bus-fare back, and a snack meal from the takeaway on the way home. Sue said, 'That's better! For a moment then I thought you were pining for our Jeremy, with that faraway look in your eyes.'

'Whatever I might pine for, if ever I do, it won't be for that conceited piece of work, I promise you, Sue.' They finished their drinks and made their way into town, where the sound of mechanical music floated on the dusky air. Bishop's Corner was a patch of waste ground where market stalls sold cheap socks and fresh vegetables on Saturdays. Tonight it was lit up with strings of coloured lights, and young people were flocking round the alleys where shooting ranges and side-shows vied with candyfloss and ice-cream stalls. In the middle were the rides, and the two friends

shouldered their way through, choosing the Big Wheel
for their first bit of excitement.

Faireholme lay beneath them, as the wheel swung
them high over the rooftops; their tidy little town,
whose shops and cafés were all well known to the two
nurses. Alanna looked down, and felt that tendril of
longing for something, she didn't know what. She
blamed Jeremy Masters for starting that seed of doubt.
Again she remembered that Jeremy had said it first.
She looked out at the horizon, where the low hills
heralded the beginning of the Lakeland mountains.
And she knew that she was eager and hopeful for
something bigger and more of a challenge than playing
badminton for her town against other small town teams,
more than working in the hospital operating theatre for
the rest of her life. Yet Faireholme was sweet, and it
was her home. And most of all, once Tim was out of
the way it was safe. . . They were both laughing,
however, as they stepped out of the gently rocking seat
as the wheel brought them at last down to earth. 'What
next?' asked Sue. 'How about the dodgems? You
always wanted to learn to drive!'

Alanna was counting out the necessary small change.
Suddenly she heard Sue give a little shriek, and looked
up to see her being lifted bodily into one of the little
cars by Sam Neill, one of the senior AED housemen.
'Hey, come back!' she laughed.

'You can come with me, Alanna.'

She recognised his voice before she turned round
and looked up into Jeremy's face. He put his hand over
hers. 'Put that money away—I've already paid.' And
she found herself being lifted into a car before Jeremy
slid into place beside her. They were very close
together, the music swelled, and his arm rested round
her shoulders as he put his foot down and steered one-

handed around the noisy arena, chasing the other couple. 'Enjoying it?' he asked, with a cheerful grin.

Somehow there was nothing for it but to sit back and join in. His embrace was not threatening, but exciting and fun. She was enjoying it, and said so. 'Even though I hardly know you!'

'That's part of the pleasure,' he replied, and gave her shoulder a squeeze. The old Alanna would have been indignant at his cheek, but she had to admit that it did make the fair a whole lot more fun to have someone to go around with. It would do no harm, one evening of innocent togetherness. And Jeremy and Sam were definitely in a mood to make the most of the fair, teasing each other, joking, and making the girls giggle. Jeremy drew Alanna to a rifle-shooting stall. 'Stand close and bring me luck,' he murmured, as he aimed for the moving targets. It was only when he had won first prize, and donated the huge fluffy panda to Alanna, that she realised they had somehow lost the other two.

'Sue will be worried——' she began.

'You don't want to spoil their evening, do you?' said Jeremy. 'Sam would really like to get to know your friend better. I think he said something about taking her for a meal.'

Alanna was by now so relaxed that she scarcely saw any threat whatsoever in Jeremy's company. 'If you're sure she won't be looking for me——'

'I know she won't. Come on, it's time we went on the Big Dipper!'

'But, Jeremy, they're all little kids up there!' she protested.

'What difference does that make? You want to go, don't you?'

She looked up into his sparkling eyes and nodded. If a famous senior registrar could let his hair down like a

cheerful schoolboy then so could Alanna. Amazed at
herself, she said, 'Why not?'

'That's my girl! Come on, then—quick!' And they
climbed into the last two seats and fastened the bar
across their knees. It was only as the miniature carriages began their slow, halting climb up to the top of
the spindly tower that Alanna realised she was again
being held in a close grip by Jeremy Masters, the
hospital Lothario, and she was loving every second of
it. So he had got his way, in spite of her unwillingness
to become involved with him. Her natural admiration
of his skill in the operating theatre had been manipulated—by the best player at the game of love in
Faireholme. The few whispered words in the corridor.
The deliberate attempt to arouse her interest and
jealousy by showing attentions to his ex-girl, Emma
Forbes—oh yes, he was skilful all right—as skilful at
breaking hearts as he was at mending bodies. If only
he realised he was dealing with the one girl who
wouldn't play his game—with the cool one.

But then her breath was forced out in a little scream,
as the carriages rounded the top, paused for a split
second, then plunged down in a heart-stopping dive.
She clung on to Jeremy, comforted and glad that his
arm was tight around her. Breathless with the stimu-
lation and excitement of the ride, she was still laughing
as she held his arm when they stepped off after the ride
was over, and she felt her knees go weak. Both his
arms went round her then, and she was held close
against the warm wool of his sweater in an embrace of
the utmost sweetness, until she found her feet again,
and realised just what he was doing. He was kissing
her, and it was incredible, because she wanted him not
to stop.

Then her fears began to ring warning bells in her

brain. 'Don't! Please don't.' She tried to push him away.

'I'm sorry, I didn't realise what I was doing. I didn't mean to, Alanna.' His face was apologetic, but one arm was still around her waist.

Alanna laughed awkwardly. 'Oh, Jeremy, I don't believe a word you say!'

'Are you calling me a liar?' The dimples in his cheeks belied his hurt tone, and as they walked away from the Big Dipper, Alanna found it easier to walk if she put her own arm around his waist too. He murmured, 'Shall we go and eat now? Had enough excitement?'

'All right.'

'You aren't mad at me?'

'I haven't decided yet. Somehow I feel there isn't much point in getting mad.'

'Good girl! Well, what shall it be? Indian, Chinese, or fish and chips?'

Later, sitting opposite to Jeremy Masters at a little pine table in a salad bar, Alanna found her voice at last. He was plainly waiting for her to speak. 'It was a lovely evening. Thank you,' she said.

'It isn't over yet. I've got to get you home.'

'I'll catch the bus, thank you.'

'But, Alanna, I'd be a cad and a heel if I allowed that.'

She smiled at him, confident now that she had regained control of her feelings, and could give him a brush-off in the politest language possible. 'You'd quite possibly be that anyway. I've heard all the stories, Jeremy, and I want to say that I'm not going to be talked about along with all the others. I'm going home alone.'

He raised an eyebrow, clearly unused to such a reply. 'You've enjoyed yourself, though?'

'Very much, thank you.' She placed her knife and

fork neatly on her empty plate. Then she picked them up again and played with them, afraid of that magnetic look. She tried to be diplomatic but honest. 'It isn't anything personal. But you're a very clever man, and I feel very much as though I'm being manipulated, and it doesn't make me very comfortable.'

'I'm sorry—I didn't mean to make you feel that. I just—I just had one of the nicest evenings of my life, Alanna, and I thought you might have had the same feeling.'

She smiled again, though her heart dipped in her breast at the sincerity in the dark blue eyes. 'Jeremy, I wonder just how many times you've said that line— with just the same little-boy look in your eyes.'

He sat up then, and looked down at his unfinished lettuce. 'I don't think it matters how many times I've said it—so long as tonight I mean it.'

She noticed that his lashes curled on the smooth cheek, and that his face was so handsome that she wanted to reach out and touch it. Could she really become one of Jeremy's scalps? At that moment she very nearly gave in, and stopped fighting him. But Alanna didn't want to fall in love. She wanted it, if it came, to be special and wonderful. Tim Howarth had implied that she was incapable of real love. Jeremy might be the one to teach her—but he had left behind him a string of casual affairs, and Alanna couldn't bear to fail again. She looked up and said softly, 'It was fun tonight.'

'It was wonderful. We get on so well, Alanna. We laugh at the same things—enjoy the same things.'

'Yes—like good friends, maybe?'

He looked into her eyes. 'That'll do for a start,' he said, as softly as she. 'And good friends don't let their mates ride home on a corporation bus.'

It wasn't easy. But Alanna knew that if she once sat

beside Jeremy in his sports car, he would have won, and she would have committed herself. So she insisted that he leave her at the bus stop. 'I always catch this bus—the conductress knows me. Goodnight, Jeremy.'

He shrugged his shoulders. This obviously didn't happen to him very often. He stood watching her as the bus drew away. Alanna, clutching a rather cumbersome panda, had a struggle with herself, but didn't turn and wave. The conductress said, 'He's smitten, love, I can see it in his eyes. Fancy going off and leaving him like that!'

Alanna put the giant panda down beside her as she took out her coins. 'No,' she said, 'he isn't smitten. He's just struck dumb because he hasn't had his own way.'

'That can't happen often! I wouldn't leave a man like that standing on the pavement, I can tell you.'

Had she really made the right decision? 'I had to.' Alanna could see that the conductress didn't believe her, but she repeated again, to convince herself, 'I just had to.'

As she let herself into the nurses' home, she saw the light colour of Sue's dress in the shadows, enveloped in Sam's arms, and a twinge of loneliness curled in her heart. After all, she was twenty-six, and apart from Tim there had been no one. She felt a longing to be held, as she had been for those few moments, held close against Jeremy's chest, and kissed like someone very precious. . . But no. She would have regretted it. She had done the right thing, coming home alone. She ran quickly upstairs to their flat, diving into bed and pulling the duvet right up over her face. As an aftrthought, she sat up and pulled the panda inside the bed with her. Some people could cope with passion, with sexual frenzy and all the misery it could create. 'And some are just good nurses. . .' She said her

prayers, secretly and silently, and was asleep when the
key turned in the lock to let Sue in.

Sue made coffee next morning. 'No one will believe
you, Al,' she said. 'Nobody has ever turned him down.'

'I nearly didn't,' Alanna admitted.

'But?'

Alanna waited until Sue turned. 'I don't want to be
hurt, Sue. I don't want to be dumped when the next
one comes along. Can you understand that? I don't
want to fail.'

Sue nodded, but clearly didn't entirely comprehend.
'I suppose I see what you're getting at. But I'm darned
if I'd have had the courage to say no to Jeremy Masters.
It's like refusing the King of England. You'll just never
have another chance.'

'That's the way I like it,' insisted Alanna.

'Aren't you operating with him this morning?'

Alanna smiled ruefully. 'Yes. Wish me luck! I hope
the chief turns up instead.' She put a brave face on
things, but felt her knees tremble slightly as Jeremy
strolled into theatre, smiled politely and nodded, then
turned round for Alanna to tie his mask and gown
before helping him on with his gloves. She smelt his
aftershave, knowing with a pang just how it felt to have
that cheek up close against her own. She took a deep
breath, and reminded herself that at least her name
wasn't being bandied about the hospital, the way
Emma Forbes' had been. Jeremy was stunning. But he
was resilient. He would very soon find himself another
companion to console his idle moments, a companion
livelier, more sophisticated, sexier. . . She must waste
no tears on what might have been. In reality she had
had a lucky escape.

They were already deep into the first operation
before Jeremy said, as he held out his gloved hand for

a retractor, 'Did you have a nice time at the fair, Alanna?'

He was trying to discomfit her, with the patient's own hip joint lying in a tin bowl, and the artificial socket being gently eased into place in the healthy femur. She wasn't going to allow him to catch her out, however her heart thumped. 'I had a wonderful time,' she answered.'

'You don't think fairs are a little childish for people of our age?'

She repressed a giggle. He did have a knack of being fun. 'Slightly, I suppose. But I don't see any harm in them. Do you?'

'I love them,' he replied with a straight face. 'There isn't much to do around Faireholme. I suppose you have the leisure centre to go to if you're bored?'

'I'm never bored,' she replied.

Jeremy looked up at her then, turning around to look into her eyes as she stood close beside his right arm. The house-officer was passing her the metal ball of the artificial hip. Again she smelt Jeremy's warmth and the man of him, and felt as though she knew, and was part of his very soul. It hurt, knowing that she wasn't. He handed her a swab to put away, as he eased the joint into its natural position, then held out his hand for suction. Almost under his breath he said so that no one else in the room could hear him, 'I wonder why those lovely eyes are so sad, then,' and turned back to his work at once, leaving Alanna to hope that her mask hid her violent blush.

After the session, with three patients in Recovery, Alanna watched him stride away, feeling at last that she could relax. The theatre nurse said, 'So it was you he met at the fair, then?'

'Yes, Sue and I ran into him—briefly.'

'Lucky old you!'

'Don't get any ideas. I'm not one of his conquests!'
That had to be made very clear. Alanna walked along
the corridor towards the room where Tim Howarth was
on the mend. She didn't really want to talk, but it was
only her duty.

His eyes brightened when he saw her. 'Alanna! I
thought you'd forgotten me.'

She stood at the foot of the bed, keeping her
distance. Her feelings were too fragile today. 'I won't
do that, Tim. Is there anything I can get you?'

'I wouldn't mind a kiss.' She looked down at him,
sensing a danger, surprised at his boldness after. . .
But Tim said, 'Just a little one?' And she moved round,
bent and kissed his cheek, feeling the roughness of his
beard, but feeling nothing else but numbness. 'Thanks,
lass. I don't get many visitors in here.'

'You ought to be out in the main ward. Have you
asked Sister? It's much more lively when there are
other people to talk to—now that you're over the
worst.'

'I was hoping—that you'd be willing to give me some
help with my exercises, as soon as the plaster comes
off.'

Sensing a plot, Alanna put on a careful smile. 'Of
course I will.' She would have to think of an excuse
later. But the poor fellow had been through a lot, and
she was too tender-hearted to refuse straight out.

'You're a brick, Al.' He was trying too hard to be
nice. 'How's the badminton coming on?'

'Fine. We're on a winning streak.' Thanks to
Jeremy's joining the team when he was off duty.

'And judo?'

'Haven't done much of that, Tim. But it's good to
know we can protect ourselves, thanks to you.'

'Maybe I can come along and give you all a refresher
course?'

She smelt danger again. 'I thought you'd want to get back to your Cumbrian fells as soon as possible,' she told him.

'Of course. But no hurry.'

'With the tourist season coming?'

'The scenery in Faireholme seems better to me at the moment.'

Alanna walked away with a sense of foreboding. Tim was hoping to start up their old friendship, and she didn't want there to be anything between them ever again. She must make sure that she encouraged all the badminton team to visit him to take his mind off himself. It was a pity that Tim hadn't found himself another girl.

'How did you find him, Alanna?'

She was getting used to seeing Jeremy suddenly appear when she was least expecting him, and not having time to put on an act, she gave him a broad smile. 'How on earth do you do it, Jeremy? Pop out of rooms and appear just like that? Are you a genie or something?'

He looked down at her, and his eyes were gentle and thoughtful. 'What a smile! You know, you're quite beautiful, Alanna, and that isn't one of my lines. Was that just for lucky old me, or did Timothy get one too?'

She looked away suddenly, embarrassed at the effect she seemed to have on him. She said more seriously, 'If we could talk about the patient—I'm not sure that it's a good thing for Tim to be by himself. Could we ask Sister to move him into the ward? Or at least have someone else in with him?'

'I'll see what I can do,' said Jeremy. 'We genies are good at granting wishes.'

'Thank you,' she said.

'And now I expect you want me to go back in the bottle?'

'I didn't say that.'

'But you do expect me to know my place, don't you, Alanna?'

She looked up at him, her eyes pleading. 'That wasn't fair, Jeremy. I've a right to say no to you if I think it's right. It doesn't mean—that I want you to disappear, you know. I'd like—to be friendly.'

'Your wish is my command, o, princess.'

'You do love to tease people, don't you!' Alanna sighed.

'Just you, princess. You have the spirit to tease me back. I never know quite what you might say, and it's intriguing me.'

She felt the force of his gaze, and longed to look up and share the beauty of it, but she dared not, very much aware of his charm, and her own weakness to resist. 'You'll soon grow out of that, I dare say,' she told him.

'Alanna, you're judging me by my reputation instead of what you yourself think of me. That isn't fair, you know. Why won't you get to know me first, before you make judgements?'

She did face him then, nervous, but trying to maintain total control. 'I stand at your side every time you operate, you know. You think I don't know you yet?'

'Not a bit.' His tone was bantering now. 'I defy you to tell me what you've learned about me by handing me scalpels and swabs!'

'I've learned plenty—some good and some bad.'

'Tell me the good first.' They were standing very close together, and she was reminded of the warmth and texture of his sweater when he had swept her into his laughing embrace last night at the fair.

'Certainly not! We can't have you growing conceited, now, can we?'

'I wish you'd give me a chance to try. You've dented my credibility, you know, Alanna.'

They exchanged a knowing look, and she felt that somehow she had penetrated below the surface. She said gently, 'That's the way I like it, Jeremy.' She didn't want to leave him, enjoying his closeness and his frankness—but she knew it was a good comment to leave him with. Maybe her rejection of him might prevent some other poor girl from becoming such an easy victim as he seemed to be used to. Maybe it was time his credibility was dented.

Alanna was on time for the badminton practice. There was a match on Saturday, so she made sure that on Wednesday evening she was ready at the nets, to make up for being absent without leave at the last practice night. Fred Hodges, captain and coach, was there with his wife, Jo, already knocking up; and for the first time in her life Alanna wondered why they did this, why they were so keen to spend all their available time training others. If I had a new husband, I'd want us to have some time together, some time not shared with a gang of sporting hopefuls. . . Now what on earth made her think that? She wasn't in any danger at all of getting a husband. In fact, the prospect was so far away that Alanna couldn't even envisage it at present. Who—or what—would she eventually fall in love with? Or would she be one of the band of females who made their way contentedly through life without finding a soulmate?

'Hello, Alanna. Hi, Fred and Jo. Do you think I stand a chance this week? I've been practising hard.' And as Alanna turned, hardly believing her ears, Jeremy Masters smiled at her, brandished his racket and said, 'It's your friendly neighbourhood genie again!'

He wore white shorts and an open-necked shirt, and before she could help it, Alanna found herself positively overwhelmed by the physical beauty of the man. Unfortunately, the only words that found a way into her mouth were, 'Oh, no, not you!' Jeremy was the only one who had heard her. He stood, totally unembarrassed, and waited until she came up to him, prepared to apologise for her thoughtless remark. He smiled, and all she could think of was how his face lit up when he smiled. She said, 'I shouldn't have said that. I'm sorry.'

Jeremy said calmly, 'It happens to me all the time. You wouldn't believe it!' And with another grin, he threw his shuttlecock into the air and batted it gently towards Jo.

Alanna stood for a moment. She had to be logical about this. There was only one reason for Jeremy Masters to turn up and show keenness at the local leisure centre, and that was because he wanted to put her in her place. She must not show any reaction at his presence, or she would have lost the round. She was aware of her own skill at badminton, so she eased herself round the net opposite to Jeremy and Jo and said, 'How about a mixed doubles to start?'

But Jeremy proved harder to beat than she had expected, and it was an exhausting game, before Alanna and Fred came out as the victors. And as they all stood breathless at the water-cooler, Jeremy said under his breath to Alanna, 'You'll have to try something else if you want to put me down, my dear.'

She smiled, wiping her forehead with a lace-edged handkerchief. 'I wouldn't dream of trying to do that. I mean, where exactly is your place? I've never quite been able to work that one out.'

Jeremy sat down on a battered plastic chair and sipped his water before looking up at her sweetly.

'Why, by your side, of course. You mean to say you didn't know that by now?'

She knew he was teasing, that he was trying his best to make her feel uncomfortable. But she didn't expect his words to have such an effect on her. When he said 'By your side' she felt an uncontrollable need to weep. Catching her breath, she muttered an excuse and ran out of the gym towards the women's lockers. She stayed there a long time. When she finally felt strong enough to face everyone again, Jeremy had gone. Fred was saying, 'It's marvellous! Just the week that Mr Roberts is away with flu, we turn up a player like Mr Masters. What luck that he's off duty, Alanna. We've found you a partner worthy of you. There's no way we can lose on Saturday now!'

Alanna felt as though there was a conspiracy closing in on her, driving her like a fox at bay towards the ultimate destiny of an affair with Jeremy Masters. And she shook her head decidedly. It would never happen. She would make sure of that.

CHAPTER THREE

TIM HOWARTH was being allowed to leave hospital. Alanna stood at the foot of his bed, realising that she didn't know where he lived. All she knew about him now was that he had very few visitors, and that he worked in Keswick as a mountain guide. He smiled up at her, his eyes wistful. 'Say you're delighted with my progress?'

'You know I am, Tim. It's miraculous, it really is. Your arm looks almost normal. If only you'd seen what a mess it was when you were brought in!'

'I'm rather glad I didn't, thank you.' He moved his wrist gingerly. 'It works fine now. Still a bit stiff, but that's getting better every day.'

'You'll be coming back for physio?' she asked.

'Oh, yes—for another four weeks. After that, your young man is talking of transferring me to a hospital near Keswick for follow-up.'

Her young man. . . There was a sarcastic sound to that, but Alanna ignored it. 'I expect when you get back on the fells you'll take extra care to take no risks,' she said.

'Funny you should say that, Al. You know, I'm wondering whether I want to go back to that type of work. Fred and Jo have asked me to go back to the sports centre. You do know I'm staying with them until the end of the month?'

The sports centre. . . Alanna murmured something encouraging. But she felt a stab of uncertainty. If Tim was planning to stick around, maybe she herself would be wise not to go so often. It would never do for him to try to warm up their old flame, that had left only bitter ashes in her life. Yet that was how it seemed. She looked at her watch. 'I'd better go—Sue will be waiting.'

'Alanna?'

'Yes?' With sinking heart she knew what was coming.

'Please may I take you out to dinner? To celebrate my freedom?'

She swallowed, unable to think of a reasonable excuse. 'Of course, Tim. Later. We'll sort out a suitable time, when you're feeling better.'

'I'm fine now.' And she could tell from the look in his eyes that he recognised her reluctance. There was a truculence in his voice. 'I'd like it to be soon, Al.'

'Sure.' She looked at her watch again. 'I'll leave you the phone number of the flat.' As she handed it over, he took her hand in his good one and held it firmly. Alanna felt waves of repugnance at the touch, and hoped it didn't show on her face.

His tone was humble. Maybe he remembered the bitter recriminations when she had thrown his engagement ring back into his face. He had a hasty temper in those days, and a rough sexual appetite. . . Alanna had been a virgin, but it had made no difference to his behaviour, the way he'd forced himself into her. 'I promise not to be a nuisance.'

Alanna almost ran back to the nurses' home. Sue was in the bathroom, singing at the top of her voice. 'Hi there, Ali! What do you think? I'm going out with Sam Neill. There's a party at the doctors' residence. Are you coming?'

Alanna lay down on her bed, absently pulling the giant panda into her arms, and staring at the ceiling. She hadn't even known that what Tim had done was called rape. . . After a long time Sue emerged from

the bathroom, her face pink and her hair and eyes
bright. 'I've had a face-pack. Can you tell the
difference?'

'Yes, you're all shiny!'

Sue threw a pillow in her direction. 'Come on, Al—
come to the party. You look fed-up. It will do you
good.'

'And play gooseberry? Not likely!'

'There'll be lots of unattached men.'

'Jeremy might be there,' said Alanna.

Sue wrapped her bathrobe firmly around her waist
and sat down on Alanna's bed. 'So what? He's as much
right as you to go to a party. Oh, come on Alanna!
You're being paranoid. I'm sure Jeremy has realised
by now that you aren't interested.'

Alanna sat up and leaned on one elbow. 'Why can't
my life be simple?' she sighed. 'Tim Howarth wants to
see me again, and I don't want to start anything with
him. And I don't want to go to the residence in case
Jeremy thinks I'm chasing him. Oh, Sue, I've had
enough of men. I think I'll join a convent.'

Sue went over to her dressing-table and began comb-
ing out her damp hair. 'It better not be a silent order!
You talk too much.' She dragged the comb slowly to
the very ends of her damp hair. 'You know, Al,' she
said thoughtfully, 'I've always been a bit jealous of
your looks and your figure. You're good at your job,
good at games and sport, and men turn to look at you
in the street. Here am I, just ordinary—and I'm over
the moon because Sam Neill has asked me out for a
second date. I feel as though fireworks are flashing and
stars are exploding. Why isn't it like that for you?'

'Because you've probably met someone who really
likes you. You're the lucky one, Sue. So advise me.
What shall I do?'

'Well, if you really want to avoid seeing Tim, why

don't you take some leave until he's gone back to
Cumbria? If he's got any sense at all he'll realise why
you've gone.'

'Brilliant! Why didn't I think of that? I'll see about it
right away. That will solve both my men problems, if I
just disappear from the scene for a week or two.'
Alanna tapped the panda on the back with renewed
relief.

'So now that you've decided that, come to the party?'

'No, thanks. I'll just grab myself some supper in the
dining-room, and watch some TV. I hope you have a
great time, Sue. See you tomorrow!'

In the hospital dining-room, a couple of weary
housemen sat nodding and silent over rapidly cooling
pizzas and tried to keep their eyes open. In the corner
the senior physiotherapist was having a vegetarian
lasagne with a tall obstetrician, and holding forth to
him about her plans for his department. He looked
bored. Two student nurses gossiped in excited whispers
over a quick coffee. Alanna took her slice of chicken
pie to a table near the window, where she could look
out at the fresh new cherry blossom along the drive,
and feel the revitalising warmth of approaching
summer. The table was drab, and the dining-room
carpet was cheap and worn. But at least there was no
hassle here. Alanna could relax, and plan her holiday,
free of Tim and free of Jeremy.

When he slid into the seat opposite, Alanna felt
herself tense up, her hands clench involuntarily round
the coffee mug. Surely, surely by now Jeremy had
found someone else to chase. Why was he still following her around? She looked across at him, ready with
a sarcastic comment. But it died on her lips as she saw
a great weariness in his face, a dullness in his usually
twinkling eyes. She said, 'You've been working until
now?' It was after nine in the evening.

He nodded. 'One of Bates' private cases. The hip was infected, and she hadn't told anyone about it. Lord, you should have seen it!' He yawned, and brushed his hair back. 'You know, I sometimes wonder if I'm in the right profession.'

'You can't mean that!' protested Alanna.

'It didn't help having old Sister Barclay in theatre instead of you. She drops half the instruments—and the other half you can hardly get hold of because her hands are shaking!'

'She's probably scared of you.' But Alanna suppressed a giggle at the mental picture of surgical instruments being scattered around the theatre. It wouldn't suit Jeremy's efficient nature at all.

He muttered, 'I wanted to ask for you, but they said you weren't answering your phone. I thought maybe you'd gone to Rick's party.'

Alanna looked down. She wouldn't tell him that she had stayed away for fear of meeting him there. 'I wanted an early night.' She looked into his face and felt sorry for wanting to avoid him. 'Can I get you something to eat?'

'No—I had a snack before operating. I have to go back to the ward to make sure this old biddy is OK before I turn in.' He smiled suddenly, and leaned forward, his elbows on the table, his face near hers. 'But I can't tell you how nice it was to spot you sitting here all alone. The one person in the world I'd rather be with.'

She didn't reply at once. What was there to say? That she wished he'd leave her alone? Somehow that didn't ring true at the moment. 'You're a strange man, you know,' she told him. 'Difficult to know—unpredictable.'

His eyes were on her. 'Wait here, I'm going for a coffee. Want one?' And in a moment he was back with two hot coffees. It was getting dark outside, and before he sat down he switched on the light over their table. 'Now tell me, Alanna, do you play poker?' And he plunged his hand into the pocket of his white coat and brought out a pack of cards. 'I'll give you a valuable lesson—teach you how to bluff. Here, we'll play for——' he looked around '—we'll play for matches.' He opened a box and spilt the loose matches on the table. 'I'll claim my winnings when I'm feeling a bit more awake!' And he shuffled the pack with hands that she knew were skilful with a scalpel, but had never seen move so quickly or so professionally before as he shuffled again, cut, and dealt. 'OK, have a look at your cards, and tell me if you're happy with them!'

'Wouldn't you be better lying down in your room?' she queried.

'No. You wouldn't come with me, and I don't want you to run away. Now, when you look at your cards, I want you to keep a perfectly straight face, whether they're good or bad.'

She started to laugh. 'This is so ridiculous, Jeremy!'

'It's fun, though, isn't it?'

Alanna had to admit it, as they played hand after hand, and Jeremy gradually acquired almost all the matches on the table. Totally relaxed, thoroughly enjoying the evening, she was surprised when the night kitchen staff put the lights off and went home. 'It's eleven already!' she exclaimed.

'And you owe me quite a lot of money, Alanna. Lucky you, that I haven't got time to collect. I've got to go back up to the ward to see my patient in Recovery. Thanks for cheering me up, love.' And he leaned across the table suddenly and kissed her on the lips, swiftly but firmly. Then he swept up the cards into a pile and put them deftly back in his pocket. 'We'll do this again some time, eh?'

She walked back to the flat, touching her lips gently, remembering his warm, sensuous kiss. What a man! As though he understood that she felt threatened by him, he had skilfully passed an entire evening with her without her feeling the slightest bit afraid. She paused at the front door and looked up at the lighted windows of his ward. Oh, Jeremy, please don't keep on being so nice to me. I really don't want to fall in love—not with you. I'd only be so terribly hurt in the end, I know I would. Because I wouldn't fall out of love—and you would, just as you always do, out of love with all your girls and on to the next, without a care in the world.

It was bound to happen—the hospital grapevine started passing the news that Jeremy Masters' latest was Alanna Keith. They played cards together. They stopped to whisper and laugh in the corridors, and in theatre they often had conversations together that nobody else could hear. Yet the grapevine was most disappointed that the couple were never seen going out together. She was never seen in his car, and if one of them went to a hospital party, the other one was never there. What sort of scandal was that, when the suspects gave no sign of caring? And when asked directly, they both denied all rumours with a vehemence that had to be believed.

Aware of the gossip, Alanna did as Sue suggested, and took ten days of her holiday, hoping that by the time she returned the entire story would have died down. She took the train home to her widowed mother and maiden aunt, who lived together in a bungalow in Blackpool. They weren't the liveliest of company, preferring their own steady lives of Women's Institute bingo, church flowers and sitting contentedly in front of the television. It was boring—but a necessary respite from being pursued by a determined Jeremy Masters, as well as dogged by an unhappy past that she didn't want rekindling. Surely when she returned to Faireholme Jeremy would have turned his attentions to someone else? There could hardly be anyone else who had the strength of mind to say no to those handsome blue eyes and that divine red Porsche.

Ten days later Alanna knew she was hurrying from the station to the hospital, and she knew why she was hurrying. She had missed him very much. There just couldn't ever be anyone quite so fascinating, quite so unpredictable, quite so desirable. . .

'Alanna! Great to see you. I was getting quite worried about you. Why did you go off without letting me know where you were?'

'Oh—hello, Tim.' Alanna hoped her disappointment didn't show in her face. She looked up at his tall frame, his sandy beard and those intense deep-set eyes. 'I—needed a break.'

'I am glad I've found you. How about dinner tonight? I've been practising driving, and my arm is practically as good as new!'

'Oh, but——'

'Here, let me carry your suitcase.' Tim took it from her, throwing his raincoat over his shoulder to do so. 'Look, I'll wait at the main gate while you change and meet me in half an hour.'

'Tim—not tonight. Please?' There was a desperation in her voice that even Tim noticed. 'I—need to settle down—see what my duty rota is, that sort of thing. Can you phone me in a few days, when things are back to normal?'

His voice hardened. 'I believe I've been quite patient already, Alanna. You promised to come out with me, and I've been looking forward to it for a long time. It isn't like you to break your promises—especially to someone who's been through a bad time.'

She stood dejected. 'Could I have my suitcase, please?' she said.

'I'll carry it up for you.'

'No—please! Tim, can't you see——'

Another voice broke in on their conversation. 'Yes, Tim, can't you see that the lady doesn't want to be bothered just now? Lay off, man! It isn't fair to pester her like that. She's just had a long journey. Be a good chap and leave her alone just now.' Jeremy stood in the evening sunlight, wearing the slacks and sweater he had worn on the night of the fair.

Firmly he took the suitcase from Tim's nerveless hand and placed it on the ground in front of Alanna. 'Off you go, Sister. He won't bother you tonight.'

Tim spoke between clenched teeth. 'So that's it! I see now—all too clearly. You want to muscle in on her yourself. Well, let me tell you, Mr Clever, just because you're working your way through the female population of this hospital, that I'm not the type to——'

Jeremy turned to Alanna and gestured towards the nurses' home. She picked up her case and fled towards the safety of its front porch, closing the door with a firm click behind her. But as she went, she heard Jeremy's reasoned tones, pointing out that he wasn't going to allow anyone to treat Sister Keith like that. Her heart was banging against her ribs when she got up to her own flat. Sue was out, and Alanna gratefully flung the suitcase on the floor and herself on the bed. The panda, who had been balanced on her pillow, tumbled over, and she took him into her arms with a hard, comforting squeeze.

She didn't see Jeremy any more until it was his turn to operate. Perhaps things would settle down now, with Tim warned off, and Jeremy taking less notice of her.

Maybe she would even meet a nice young man like Sam, and have a normal relationship at last. She made her way to the theatre with renewed hope, glad to be back at work.

Jeremy was already there. 'Hi, Alanna.' His eyes were as fascinating and warm as ever. 'You OK now? No more bother from our mountaineering friend?'

'No—thanks to you, Jeremy. It was kind of you——'

'I did it for a reason.' A knowing look that made her catch her breath. 'Would you help me with these gloves?'

As she moved closer to him, she knew very well that her feelings had strengthened, if possible, during her holiday. She held the powdered gloves for him, wondering if he could tell that the blood was pounding in her ears, and she could think of nothing at all to say. What reason did he have? Was he going to tell her?

But during the operation he said very little, merely pointing out to his houseman how expensive artificial joints were getting, and how there ought to be more competition among manufacturers to bring hospital costs down. 'It's the old story, Simon—the more sophisticated medicine becomes, the more there's need for it. How long can we go on giving wealthy people new hips and hearts and kidneys, when in the Third World there's still no clean water? I'm afraid that as surgeons we can't do much about the problem, unless we care so much that we go and work in the Third World.'

'Have you ever thought of doing that?' asked the other man.

'To be honest, yes. But I'll need to get a consultancy first, and a couple of years' more experience.'

Alanna listened, full of admiration. Womaniser he might be, but perhaps his reluctance to settle down was something to do with his ambition to eventually go somewhere where his skills could be better used. Perhaps she had been so concerned about being hurt herself that she had been blind to the real, caring Jeremy. She saw it more clearly today, as his steady eyes looked down at his patient, and his steady voice spoke of noble works. This was the man who had held her on the Big Dipper, laughed with her as they bumped their way round the dodgems, sat with her playing a mean game of poker and joking about her lack of ability to keep a straight face. This was the real Jeremy Masters, and she knew that nothing could ever come of loving him.

After the operating session, she changed and started to make her way to the dining-room. Sue had arranged to meet her there, as Sam was away doing a two-day course in Lancaster. She felt calm and peaceful, as the sun streamed in, and the hospital grounds outside looked fresh and summery. It was satisfying to know she understood Jeremy thoroughly at last, and she wondered if he had known how intently she was listening to and admiring his conversation that morning.

She worked for a different surgeon in the afternoon. Funny how his compliments on her efficiency sounded ordinary, when she had glowed with pride in the morning when Jeremy had merely said, 'Very well done, Ali.'

She showered when she got back, and changed into jeans and a cotton sweater while she waited for Sue to come off duty. With Sam away, it seemed a nice idea for them to resume their table at the Robin's Nest, and have a leisurely drink outside just as they used to. But when the flat bell rang it was Jeremy, looking kind, familiar, powerful. Sue would understand if the flat was empty when she came up. Somehow Alanna couldn't think of an excuse. . .

'I've never asked you this, Ali, but will you have dinner with me tonight?'

'Yes, thank you.'

He beamed. 'So you've finally overcome your distaste for my flashy sports car?'

She laughed. 'There never was any distaste for the car, and you know it. It was only caution! The terrible reputation of its owner, you know.'

'And what made you overcome your caution?' They were walking across the hospital grounds towards the car park, and Jeremy casually linked his arm through hers as they walked. Alanna forgot that she worried about what people thought, felt as though she had known him a very long time.

She said quietly, as he opened the door for her, 'I don't think one last time will ruin my reputation.'

'Last time?' he echoed. 'What are you saying? Surely you mean first time? I thought when I saw you in Theatre this morning that the signals were that you were changing your mind about me.'

'Not changing. I've always thought you were the nicest person I've ever met.' She felt strong enough to tell the truth and still resist him.

'Really?' He bent and kissed her cheek. 'Always?'

'Oh, yes, always.' It seemed the time to be frank.

'Yet you kept me at arm's length, Ali. Why?'

They were driving into the country, and the beech trees were in their finest early summer green. She didn't answer his question, and for a while they drove in silence, until they reached a secluded little inn, where Jeremy found a corner table where they couldn't be overheard. He ordered fine pale sherry, and raised his glass to her before he sipped. His eyes were serious now, but he didn't press her to speak. He said conversationally, 'You really are superlatively beautiful.'

She smiled and changed the subject. 'You've been at Fareholme nearly four years now, haven't you? Apart from working your way through the female population, you must have applied for a consultant's job by now. Will it be far from here?'

'I don't know. I haven't made up my mind yet.' Honestly he looked into her eyes. 'Is that the answer to my question, Ali? Is it because I'd be going away soon that you never—that we never——'

'I didn't think it mattered much to you. The famous Mr Masters was never short of female company. You were such fun to be with. It's only since I came back from my holiday that I feel I want to explain—because I think you'd understand, and—because you may not be around much longer.'

His eyes were dark and unreadable, and his voice was deep. 'Did you miss me? I missed you very much.'

She nodded. 'And it was only ten days. So you see why I didn't want to let myself fall for you? At first I thought— well, that I didn't want to be just one of a series! But later I thought maybe you weren't like that after all. Only that a real relationship wasn't part of your great plan.'

'Oh, thank you very much. You gave me credit at last for possibly having the ability to be faithful?'

'We haven't known each other very long, remember,' she reminded him.

'Does that make a difference? I fell for you the moment I saw your pretty eyes above that mask.'

Alanna sipped her drink, not quite sure how to go on. 'You must see that I'm quite a serious person underneath. I'd never had such good times as I had with you. But I'm so scared of being hurt, you see. I'm not sure if I could cope with it when it comes.'

Jeremy's dark blue eyes were sincere. 'It doesn't have to come, Ali. Believe me.' He reached out and held her hand tightly.

She shook her head. 'It will, I know it will. And it would be devastating when it came—if I felt as though I sort of—belonged to you, and you suddenly went away——'

'Alanna——' he squeezed her hand again '—what sort of reason is that? Any couple might be unhappy at some unspecified date in the future. So they should deny themselves any happiness now? That's what you're saying, isn't it?'

'It might sound silly to you, but I'm not as wordly-wise as you are.' Yet she had an unhappy history. Would it be wise to tell him? 'I was engaged once.' She paused, but he didn't speak. 'The break-up was terrible and bitter. So I began to hold back from relationships, hoping that one day I'd meet someone who wouldn't leave me feeling that I'd somehow failed. I hope you see now why you're wasting your time on me.'

The waiter came to take their order. Jeremy chose roast beef for them both, and ordered a bottle of claret. While they waited for the meal, he talked of other things, with that touch of humour that made all his conversations worth hearing, made him such a delight to be with. Alanna said sadly, 'I wish we could go to the fair again.'

'Life isn't all fairs, I'm afraid, love. But I'll never forget that night either. It was very special. Especially you walking away from me like a little princess and climbing on to that great bus. You were the only passenger too!' They had reached a point where they could laugh again, and she was grateful. She teased him about his skill with cards, said that it showed an ill-spent life. And Jeremy joined in the teasing, point-

ing out that she was obviously a bad sort, as she had
never paid her gambling debts.

He stopped the car before they reached the hospital.
He drew in to a country layby and switched off the
engine. He put an arm along the back of her seat. 'Ali,
I want to say that—if you feel unsure of me, then I
could prove it to you.' He paused. 'We could get
married——'

'No!' She snapped out the word. 'No, we couldn't!'
Her voice rose. She was silent for a while, realising the
enormity of his words. 'You—have a lot of decisions
to make about the future. It would be very wrong to
saddle yourself with responsibility at this stage in your
life. It——'

'Saddle?' His voice was low. 'Darling Alanna, it
would make me blissfully happy to know I could come
home to you for the rest of my life. I mean it, truly I
do.'

'I'll always appreciate you asking—and the sweet
way you said it. I appreciate it very much. But be
honest, please, Jeremy. Did you think of marriage
before tonight?'

He smiled then. Dusk was falling, but she saw the
outline of his face, and reached out a hand to touch his
cheek, as she had so often wanted to do. He caught
her hand and held it against his warm face. 'I wanted
to be with you as long as I've known you. . .you're
right, of course, darling. Loving you as much as I do, I
still do have to go away. . .'

'I know.'

'But not with another woman! Surely you must
believe me that it would be work that took me away,
never another woman, as long as I live.'

She looked down, and her fingers meshed together.
'Don't make any promises. Stay the way you are,
Jeremy, until you know your own mind. I made

promises once, and broke them all. I hurt someone very badly indeed—and he hurt me. I've never seen such hurt.'

'You were a kid—you must have been only a teenager. I'm different——'

'Jeremy, I haven't got words to tell you how much——' She stopped herself quickly. What on earth was she doing, admitting to this Romeo how much he meant to her? 'Don't make commitments—not now. Not knowing that the whole world is out there waiting for you, and that very soon we'll both probably have new friends and new surroundings. That's the way it goes.' She forced herself to smile, and suddenly wished she weren't quite so strong-minded! 'You're a typical charmer, you know that? Go on swanning through life. You'll soon forget Fairholme existed.'

He paused, and an owl hooted in the pines above them. 'You're very strong for a little slip of a girl, do you know that, Ali? Strong and true. I can see how desperate that other man must have been when you broke up, losing you. I bet he still hurts.'

'Yes, I know he does.' If only she dared confide in Jeremy. But she had never put into words what happened with Tim, and Jeremy was the last person she wanted to know her secret nightmare.

'You know?' It was dark now, as he looked at her, but she saw he suddenly realised something. 'It was Tim Howarth, wasn't it? I should have known—it showed in his eyes. I wondered why he pestered you. You were engaged to that man—for a while he must have thought you belonged to him. . .' He turned away, and his voice was suddenly low, tired, kind. 'Poor guy!'

CHAPTER FOUR

THERE were no more invitations from Jeremy. No more evenings of light-hearted fun, or whispered jokes in theatre. They spoke only of hospital matters, of patients, and improvements that could be made in the operating theatres. Alanna felt empty inside, but she felt a kind of triumph too, because she had saved herself from a bitterly broken heart and from the gossipy sympathy of three-quarters of the staff at Faireholme.

'Thank you, Sister.' After a particularly difficult operating session, she could see that even Jeremy's resilience had been worn down by the complications of a badly bleeding leg artery. She had worked beside him as he sought the source of the bleeding, swabbing the area while the houseman held on to the clamps for dear life, and Jeremy examined every millimetre to find where blood was escaping, spurting out over the bone he had just set so expertly. He anastomosed the artery, putting in a dacron tube to strengthen his repair. They all stood back, dazed with effort, and congratulated him. But to Alanna, all he said was, 'Thank you, Sister.'

She knew she deserved his coldness. And Sue was scathing. 'You're being very stupid, Ali. Can't you see that you could be having a good time with Jeremy? You said yourself what fun he was, and how much you want to be with him.'

'You don't have to spell it out, Sue. But it wouldn't be fun any more. I'd just be holding my breath, waiting for him to tell me it was over, crying through the laughter. I'm doing the right thing—I know I am. I—I couldn't stop myself falling for him, and I know it. So isn't it better not to start anything?'

'Well, if you say so. But he looks pretty grim these days as well. I know he took Emma Forbes out twice last week. But he still strides about the corridors like Dr Death.'

'I know,' said Alanna miserably. She had seen the loneliness in his eyes too, and felt guilty for being half the cause of it.

She was sitting alone in the common-room, watching the news on television. It was ten at night, almost three months after she had parted from Jeremy with a single long clinging embrace. She thought of that hug almost every night—as though neither of them could help it, really. She had felt his heart beating, and leaned her cheek against the warmth of his skin beneath the thin shirt, knowing the sadness of being close to someone who would never belong to her in the way she wanted. Now she was watching the screen, but hearing nothing of what the news-reader was saying when someone came up and sat beside her on the sofa. 'Alanna?'

He was wearing a suit and smart tie, and his curly hair was neatly brushed. She gave a slight smile, controlled her wildly beating heart, and said, 'You look like a consultant tonight, Jeremy.'

'That's what I wanted to tell you—before anyone else did. I'm going abroad to work. I've got the consultancy I wanted! It is a fantastic post—and working with the best surgeon in south-east Asia.'

It was almost a relief to know. 'At last! I knew that was what you wanted. You must be very pleased. I'm happy for you.'

'Do you think you'd like to come with me?' he asked. 'To the Far East? They need well-qualified nurses too—I asked.' His eyes were averted, as he seemed to be trying to phrase the question in a casual and non-threatening way. He seemed, too, to be holding his breath, waiting for her answer.

Alanna shook her head at once, surprised that he could even ask. 'I couldn't—I don't want to leave England. All that heat, and mosquitoes and scorpions and things. I've always liked it here. I'm not ambitious like you.'

He looked at her, and she faced him, sincerely. 'So you still think I'm bad news, Ali? Even now? You wouldn't like to work with me?'

'Especially now. You're a free spirit, Jeremy, and I'm—well, I'm the opposite. I'm—the leading player at the local badminton club.'

He stood up then and buttoned his jacket. 'And that's as far as you want to go? Well, I tried. Goodbye, then, Alanna. I don't believe you know yet what you want in life—what I read in your eyes the first time we met. One day you'll know what I mean. I—hope you'll find what you're looking for, Ali, I really do.'

She said wanly, 'So you'll be living on the opposite side of the world. That figures! A world apart—I think I always knew we were.' She stood up too. 'I do wish you well—you know that, don't you?'

'Yes, I do know that.' He looked at her, then tilted her chin so that their faces were very close together. 'And now I'm the one to walk away and get on that bus alone, eh? Goodbye, Alanna. I——' He couldn't find any more words. He took a deep breath, but didn't speak. Instead, he took a step back, twisted on his heel, and strode from the room.

She was grateful that he had given her the news first. She was able to control her expression as the buzz went round the hospital. Jeremy Masters is going to be a consultant in Singapore! Alanna said nothing. She had always known that their friendship would end. She wasn't sorry to have known him, to have experienced some moments of true happiness with him. She had always known he would move on. It was just Jeremy. It was a relief to be able to get on with her life, and put the disturbing, impetuous, talented young consultant out of her mind as much as possible.

Fred was mildly irritated with his star player. 'Your mind isn't on your tactics, Alanna. Come on, now, concentrate! You and Jo have the hardest match next week—the North of England champions, no less.'

'I realise that, Fred. Sorry. Shall we start the game again?'

'You know you're capable of beating them, don't you, lass?'

'I do. And we will, don't you worry, we'll give them a match they won't forget in a hurry!' But her brave words belied her feelings. Suddenly the leisure club appeared a sad and lonely place. Mr Roberts made a boring partner, after the fun she had had playing with Jeremy Masters. The spark had gone from her game, and she was glad to yield up the court to the reserve pair and slip away to the café for orange juice in a plastic carton.

Jo followed her. 'There's something wrong, Alanna.'

'No, not really. Everyone has their off-days, don't they, Jo?'

'Why don't you forget the practice tonight, then, and go off to town to enjoy yourself? Tim Howarth's at a loose end, and I know he's hoping you'll go to the new film at the Classic with him.'

'He asked you to say that, did he?' said Alanna drily.

'No, he didn't. But I'm a woman, Alanna, I see things that men don't. I know he's unhappy, and he'd like to make it up with you.'

Slightly amused at Jo's worldly wisdom, Alanna

excused herself from the practice. But she didn't phone
Tim. After the way Jeremy had disposed of Tim last
time, she'd hoped he wouldn't bother her again.
Anyway, Jeremy had been right when he told Tim to
lay off. Alanna had finished with Tim a long time ago,
and the pain had lasted until last year. Now she was
going through an even greater anguish of mind and
spirit over Jeremy, and all she wanted was to forget
both men and go back to being the simple, cheerful
theatre sister at Faireholme, who loved her job, and
wanted nothing better than to go on doing it without
any disturbing complications.

Francis Bates was the next person to complain about
Alanna's absent-mindedness., 'For an efficient sister,
my dear, you've just given me a scalpel when I asked
for scissors. That's rather a basic mistake, isn't it,
love?'

'I'm most terribly sorry.' Just because the operation
was over, and he only wanted her to snip the suture at
the end of the wound, it didn't make it any more
excusable to give the surgeon the wrong instrument.
She blushed fiercely, and forced herself to concentrate
on every word from then on. How could she compro-
mise her reputation like that, after years of doing
everything right, and being proud of it?

It was a month later when Francis Bates spoke to
her in the corridor. 'Oh, Alanna, could you spare me a
moment in my room later?' And when she presented
herself, hoping that he didn't have any further mistakes
to blame her with, she was surprised to see him reading
a blue air-mail letter and looking very serious. He laid
the letter on his desk, and she saw at once that it wasn't
in Jeremy's writing. That was something of a relief.
'Come in, my dear. I believe young Masters did
mention to you that the Imperial Hospital were quite
short of highly qualified nurses?'

She swallowed a sudden lump in her throat, and her reply was a little husky. 'Yes, he did mention it.'

'He asked you if you'd like a job out there?'

'Yes, he did, sir.'

'Can you tell me why you refused one? You don't need to if you don't want to, but if you would gratify my curiosity?'

'I don't see why not, sir. I'd just never thought of it. I never wanted to leave Faireholme. I'm happy here.'

'That's very nice to know. I wonder if he mentioned that the pay is four times what you get here?'

'Gosh!' She was already on top grade pay. Four times that wouldn't be chicken feed. 'He didn't mention the pay, sir—but I still wouldn't want to leave England for somewhere strange, and probably too hot, and with mosquitoes and crocodiles and things.'

'I've always known you to be a very strong-minded girl, in your own quiet way, Alanna,' said the surgeon.

'So why did you want to see me, Mr Bates?' she asked.

He indicated the letter on his desk. 'My old friend Professor Kwan Ho Kai has asked me if I would personally ask you to go and take a six-month contract with him. Apparently Masters more or less told him you were the best. Ho Kai likes to have the best.'

'But—you're asking me to leave here? To go off to Singapore just like that? When I just told you I didn't want to?'

'Hold on, love! I'm not asking you to go. And not for ever—he only wants you for six months, to train a few of his own nurses. I'd miss you like blazes, and you know damn well I would! No, Alanna, it isn't like that. I'm just doing what my old friend the Prof asked me to do—put the facts before you. That's it—I've done that. That's all. Good afternoon, my dear.'

Alanna walked slowly back to the nurses' home. High

summer was over, and the full green foliage in the hospital trees was beginning to rustle as it turned brown at the edges. Professor Kwan Ho Kai—even the name sounded too outlandish for words. Alanna couldn't begin to imagine the Imperial Hospital, the foreign faces of the patients, the sunshine, the palm trees, the impressively wealthy surgeons, and the large pay packets handed out to women with her qualifications. . .

'Alanna?'

She turned, to see the chunky shoulders of Tim Howarth in a Scandinavian sweater, his bearded face, his strong legs encased in jeans, and most of all, that intense, hangdog look in his pale blue eyes. It had been easy to avoid Tim during the summer, as the badminton club had been on holiday. She had really been hoping he would have gone back to the Lake District by now, to his mountain rescue and rock-climbing centre. But clearly he had decided in favour of sticking around Fareholme. Alanna hid a sigh. She didn't want to be rude to him, but she had no intention of renewing their friendship.

She paused and allowed him to catch up with her. His face was almost pathetically grateful. 'Hi. How have you been?'

'OK.' What else could she say? She hadn't felt back to her usual sparkling self yet, although it was over four months since Jeremy Masters had vanished from her life. Four months—nearly five. She had wondered if he would write to her at first. But after the way she had turned him down, it didn't really make any sense. He would be making his new dazzling career, the way she had always known he would—probably breaking a few more hearts on the way. He would soon have forgotten all about modest little Fareholme, and modest little Alanna. . .

'Still mooning over that big-headed surgeon?'

Her eyes blazed suddenly. 'You ungrateful oaf, Tim Howarth! The man who saved your hand—saved your career, and you dare to call him big-headed! If anyone in the world had a reason to be proud of his skill, it's Jeremy Masters, and the reason he was confident was that he knew damn well he was the best, and he wasn't a hypocrite who went round pretending he was a wimp. You ought to be thoroughly ashamed of yourself!'

Tim appeared taken aback. 'I say, hold on, lass! I didn't mean—I called him that only because I was jealous of him, that's all. I know I don't come anywhere near him in your eyes. But, Al, he's gone off to seek his fortune—and I'm here, and you're here, and we're both lonely. . .'

'I'm not lonely at all. I'm finding my work very full and satisfying, and I'm glad there hasn't been any badminton nights, because it was all getting a bit too much for me!'

He didn't reply at once. She tried not to look at the longing in his eyes. The leaves rustled above their heads, and a rather startled magpie flew out of the bushes and across the avenue. One for sorrow. Alanna realised she had been shouting. Tim said quietly, 'Let's go for a drink—just one? For old times' sake?'

She knew one drink would do no harm, and perhaps it was time for her to make up her quarrel with Tim. He appeared contrite, subdued. Surely it would do no harm to be friendly? 'All right. I've nothing else on hand just now.'

'Great! I've got a car. I think it would do you good to talk. You've been bottling up a heck of a lot, haven't you?'

'What makes you say that?' she asked.

'The way you let fly just now.' He reached for her arm as they walked towards the hospital gates, but she shook him off the moment he touched her. 'Sorry.'

'I'll come for a drink, Tim, but I'm not going to confide anything to you, you know. Let's get things straight from right now—Jeremy Masters was never anything but a friend to me, and I don't mind his going away one little bit. In fact, I'm glad he's gone. Glad he's finding somewhere a little more high-powered. Everyone knew he had the talent for better things. It was only a matter of time before he went, and we all knew that.'

'I realise that.' Tim was learning tact. 'No mentioning Masters, then. Except to say that I'll always be grateful to him for what he did for me.'

Mollified, Alanna asked, 'Why didn't you go back to Keswick as soon as you were well?'

'I think you know the answer to that one.' Tim didn't take his eyes off the road or his hands from the steering wheel, but she felt the force of his renewed affection for her, and she recoiled from it. He said, 'I don't intend to make a nuisance of myself, Al, but I did hope we could see each other now and then. You can't live like a nun.'

Alanna said quietly, 'After what you did to me, you have no right to tell me how to live.' She began to realise just how he had injured her, not only bodily, but psychologically, making her fear her woman's natural instincts, making her repel the only man she had ever loved because of the fear of being hurt again. Suddenly she had a vision of the winter to come—long dark nights, miserable wind and rain, frost, snow—and all the time Tim's pale-eyed devotion, his phone calls and suggestions, his hopeful resurrection of her one-time hero-worship. Faireholme began to appear less fair.

They managed to have a conversation of sorts in the Robin's Nest. Tim told tales of his life as a rock-climber, and the excitement of reaching the top of a

particularly difficult climb. He mentioned being asked
if he would like to go to the Alps, with a possibility of
climbing in the Himalayas later. 'But this fall and
operation put a stop to that,' he explained.

'Really? You mean you won't try again?'

'Not really. I know I'm in good shape—but there's
still some slight weakness in the muscles of the hand,
and I'd be very wrong to join an expedition, knowing
that I was the weak link in the chain. It wouldn't be
right for anyone to have to hold his life in my hands.'

'But—the Lake District?' queried Alanna.

'A man's life might be in my hands even there. Some
of those rock-climbs are murder if you don't know
them.'

She paused, feeling sorry for him, as he intended.
'So you wouldn't ever go back? I'm sorry.'

'Thanks for that, Al. I appreciate it. You know what
I think? I think we took our friendship too quickly. We
should have stayed friends. We understood one
another so well—we liked being together. We rushed
into—well, making things serious.'

Alanna's response was immediate and passionate.
'Are you blaming me, Tim? I think the rush was all on
your side. In fact, now that I know a bit more about
life—well, I can see very clearly that I was far too
young, and that you took a cruel advantage of my
infatuation.' Visions long since suppressed began to
flash into her consciousness, of his naked body writhing
over hers, the great thing between his legs looking
enormous, threatening. . .

'You were as keen as I was——'

'Stop it, Tim!' Her voice was suddenly sharp and
hurt. 'I think we'd better go back to Faireholme.'

He was quick to apologise. 'Sorry. I won't say
another word. Maybe it would have been better if I'd

been taken to a different hospital to be patched up. Seeing you again has brought everything back.'

'For me too, and I don't want to remember. We made the right decision to split up, and you know it. Don't pretend you're still coming to terms with it.'

He said, with a sincerity glowing from his eyes that reminded Alanna of a devoted Labrador, 'We had something once. We were both too eager—OK, I was. But I'd appreciate the chance of taking you out—with no strings, obviously.'

Memories of his sexual excesses, practised upon a young Alanna who didn't know what was right and what was frigid, surfaced again, and she stood up, unwilling to spend another moment in his company. 'Please, I have to get back.'

'Of course.' He sounded miserable. They drove back, and he parked close to the high stone wall near the hospital grounds. By this time Alanna's memory was no longer hidden, and the entire frightening experiences of Tim's attentions began to clarify in her mind, like a long-forgotten film coming into focus. She watched with a petrified sense of apprehension as he turned off the engine, and pulled the handbrake hard, with his good hand. There was a sudden silence, in which her fears echoed around the dark night like a warning siren.

'Goodnight, Tim.' She reached for the handle.

'Goodnight. May I pick you up tomorrow?'

'No. I'm working late.'

'I don't mind waiting.'

'No! No, Tim!'

Fully aware now of the strength of her distress, Tim said nothing more that night, except, 'That's OK, then, love. I'll see you soon, maybe?'

'I'm sure we'll—run into one another.' Alanna felt stifled, suddenly terribly anxious to get into her own flat and turn the bolt. It was a relief to lock the world out, to fling herself on the bed in her own room, and enfold the panda into her trembling arms.

'Hi, Alanna!' Sue was in the kitchen. 'Had a nice time?'

'Sure. Yes, it was all right.'

'There's some mail for you.'

Alanna switched on the bedside lamp. Sue had placed the letters by the bed, and she selected the one in her mother's writing first. She scanned it anxiously— Mum so seldom wrote. Then it became obvious why. 'Auntie Mabel and I decided to sell the bungalow and go into a sheltered flat. But when the men came, they found all the woodwork was rotten, and said we'd get nothing for the bungalow until we'd replaced all the windows and doors, and had a damp-course put in. It was a shock, love, as you'd imagine. We've no savings, and we're not quite sure what to do, except stay here, as we're really very comfy, and had no idea all this was going on under our feet.'

Alanna rifled through the papers in her 'business' drawer, and found her building society book. Mum would need every penny she had. She began to feel guilty for taking out that hundred pounds for a cocktail dress six months ago. It had been an extravagant whim, and Alanna knew she had bought it when Jeremy Masters first began to show an interest in his modest Sister Keith. What foolishness! Alanna counted her money carefully. She could let her mother have her savings, but any hope of a home of her own would have to wait another year or so. She laid the bank book on the table. There was no way Mum would have to beg. That money was as good as on its way to her.

She opened the second envelope. Inside was a note from Francis Bates, accompanying a large, impressive application form. She read the note first. 'Sorry to press you, but Professor Kwan Ho Kai has sent this, in the hope that I can find him a suitable candidate. As I do feel this is a superb opportunity for you, I've taken the liberty of enclosing a reference, in case you decide to take up this offer. Do let me know if you decide in favour.'

It was an application form for the Singapore clinic where Jeremy worked. Alanna clenched her fingers, wrinkling the paper, before she noticed the annual salary for a fully qualified theatre sister. Then her eyes popped, and she hastily smoothed out the form. A few months in the Imperial would set her savings right back where they were—and she could still help Mum and Auntie with their dry rot. The whole idea became suddenly very much more inviting. So what if Jeremy Masters was there? She could live her own life, earn some money, and come back to Faireholme when the financial matters were all sorted out. She leaned back against the pillows, hugging her panda while she thought hard.

The telephone rang in the hall. She could hear Sue answer it. 'Al! It's for you.'

Alanna came out of her room. Sue was in an all-in-one pink woolly leisure suit. 'You look like Andy-Pandy!' Alanna laughed.

Sue grinned. 'Never mind me. Go and talk to your admirer!'

Alanna picked up the receiver. 'Hello?' Who could possibly be calling at after eleven?

'Alanna, how are you?' It was Jeremy Masters, and the shock made her feel faint. 'Just wanted to say hello.'

Her hand was trembling violently. She hated Tim Howarth for making her afraid of men, especially this kind, good man. She wanted to be with him at that moment, feel his comforting embrace, hear his gentle, soothing voice talking common sense. . . If she went to Singapore, she couldn't bear the thought of starting up any relationship again with anyone, least of all Jeremy Masters. It would break her heart all over again. Slowly she replaced the receiver without saying anything.

Sue said, 'Who was that? Wrong number? It didn't sound——'

'You know very well who it was.'

'Oh, dear! Sorry for breathing.'

'Sorry, Sue. But—oh, look, it's lots of things. I have to tell you. Tim's getting heavy. I have to get away from him.' Alanna took a deep breath. 'In fact, I'm taking another job. I'm going abroad, Sue, to Singapore. I need to—just for six months or so, to make some money. Mum needs help to put the bungalow to rights. Jeremy works at the same hospital, but I want him to be quite clear that I'm not going because of him.'

Sue opened her eyes very wide, but only said, 'I get it.'

'That's all it is, Sue.'

Her friend nodded. 'I know that, Al, and so do you. But does Jeremy?'

'Jeremy doesn't even need to know I'm there. Why do you think I hung up on him? This is between Professor Kwan Ho Kai and myself. Do I make myself clear?'

'As crystal, Alanna.'

CHAPTER FIVE

'WELCOME to Singapore.' Alanna knew the voice at once. Weary after the flight, she had landed at night at Changi airport. So many passengers seemed delighted to be there. She felt isolated, as they smiled and joked, and looked forward to seeing relatives. She felt very far from home. Her feet had swollen, after so many hours in the air, and she struggled to squeeze them into the stylish sandals she had bought for her arrival. She collected her hand luggage, hoping that the Imperial Hospital had sent someone, as they had promised to meet her and take her straight to her quarters in the nurses' home.

The airport was an incredible surprise—cool air, wonderful architecture, exciting smells of exotic foods and perfumes, and a great atmosphere of space. Alanna felt very small indeed, and a certainty that whoever was sent to meet her couldn't possibly find her amongst all this luxury and grandeur, all these hundreds of people.

'Excuse me.' She turned, as she reclaimed her suitcase. 'Welcome to Singapore,' said Jeremy Masters.

'Jeremy!' What else could she say? Over all the miles, and all her problems, suddenly there was no one else in the world but Alanna facing Jeremy Masters. A new Jeremy Masters, in a white shirt and trousers, bronzed almost beyond recognition, but the deep blue eyes under the mop of curly brown hair suddenly, heart-stoppingly familiar and wonderful to see again. 'Hello.' Her voice seemed to come from far away.

'Hi, Alanna.' He lifted her case as though it weighed

nothing. He sounded matter-of-fact, almost offhand. 'Surely this isn't all you brought?'

'That's all, Jeremy. I'm not staying for long.'

He smiled down at her. Yet he wasn't the same as when they had worked togther in Faireholme. His smile was aloof and distant. He belonged here—while Alanna felt like a small-time visitor. He was a consultant, while she was a part-time visiting nurse. He was at home here, totally at home and at ease—while Alanna felt distinctly uncomfortable in spite of the air-conditioning. Her misgivings redoubled. She ought not to have come. Especially after hanging up on him when he had phoned her. Thank goodness it was only for six months. Because Jeremy's old black magic was already seeping back into her soul, and she knew it was going to be painful to live with, knowing that he wouldn't have changed, that he would already have caused a few female hearts to beat faster in the East, just as he had in the West. It was inevitable. That was just the way he was, and she had to acknowledge that a man of his charisma wouldn't alter. Jeremy said, 'The Prof asked me if I'd like to meet you—make you feel at home.'

'It's very nice of the Prof.'

Jeremy paused at the doors, as they automatically opened for the two of them to emerge into the dark tropical heat of a Singapore evening. Alanna felt suddenly swamped, overwhelmed by the humidity, the bright lights, the outlined palm trees against a navy blue sky studded with a million stars. She wiped her brow, as it began to sweat, and was conscious of her clothes sticking to her body, and her sandals still tight over her swollen feet. More than anything, she was aware of Jeremy, looking cool and collected—and of the moments of intimacy they had once shared, in that tiny hospital over on the other side of the globe. She wondered if he ever even thought of those moments, now that he was established in the sort of sophisticated lifestyle he was always destined for.

He turned suddenly, causing her to lose her step and stumble. Putting her case down, he reached for her hands and steadied her. 'It's been a long trip. You wait here, love, and I'll go and get the car.'

He was still holding her hands. They seemed to stand for an age, looking, for the first time in many months, into one another's eyes. For an instant he allowed her to see through, into his soul, and she recognised depth and passion and adventure that spoke to something inside herself. But in the next second his eyes were unreadable, and she had to be content with the superficial smile on the handsome face, unreflected in his eyes. She nodded. 'I'll wait.'

She watched his lithe steps as he vanished into the heat of the night among the thousands of cars. Above, the airport lights were bright, the Changi tower floodlit, as she had seen in in pictures. It was such a huge place. Already she was beginning to regret leaving Faireholme. Singapore was a much bigger hazard than the Big Dipper at the fair. But did Jeremy still care enough to protect her, or was she really on her own now? Pulling herself together, she reminded herself firmly that yes, she was definitely on her own, that was the way she wanted it, and it was only for six months. She drew back her weary shoulders. Then she opened her eyes wide, as a long, shiny limousine drew up beside her and Jeremy jumped out to pick up her luggage. He opened the passenger door. 'It isn't a Porsche—but it isn't a bad little runabout,' he smiled. 'We drive on the same side as in England, so you won't feel strange about that.'

As he drove out of the huge car park, and the limousine's air-conditioning blew cool vapours to ease her discomfort in the heat, she said quietly, 'I feel very strange already, as though you're a stranger—that I'm meeting you for the first time.'

Jeremy didn't reply at once. When he did, his voice sounded strained. 'I hope you didn't feel unwelcome. But—well, as from our last meeting—and telephone call—I thought unlimited hugs and kisses might just be out of place.'

Alanna felt relieved. He was making their relationship a business one, and it suited her. 'I'm very grateful to you for taking the trouble to meet me,' she said politely.

'No trouble. I volunteered, you know.'

'You're very kind. I'm flattered. The Prof sounds very nice. I know you must be happy here.'

'Thanks for asking.' He turned briefly, as they paused at a traffic light in the bustling town centre. Their eyes met, and again there was a glimpse of the man she knew, before the shield came down again. 'Yes, this was a good move. I feel as though I've made the right career decision.'

Alanna studied him, as he wove the car skilfully through the busy traffic. Yes, Jeremy was happy here. He had made no commitments in Faireholme— because he never intended to stay in one place. Alanna had been offered the chance of being just one of his lovers—and she had refused. Where did that leave her? Just like all the others—in his past. The difference was that she retained her heart and her pride. She hadn't ever allowed it to be broken, not really broken. She took a deep breath of cooled Singapore air, and was glad she had stayed aloof from him.

Weary and jet-lagged as she was, she still could not sit back, as Jeremy drove into the main arterial road, from the East Coast Highway into the vibrant explosion of light and colour that was Singapore City. What a place! What sights to see, and what beaches to explore.

For a small-town girl, she would soon be living like a jet-setter, and she was suddenly not afraid any more, but excited and eager. Singapore was a brief episode in her life—and it was only for financial purposes that she had come. But it promised to be anything but dull. She thought again of that roller-coaster at Fareholme Fair. Jeremy had been with her then. Now, although he was going to be around, Alanna knew that she could negotiate this fairground alone, that she would get home intact and with her self-confidence all in one piece.

'Well, here we are. This is the nurses' home. Want me to see you in?'

She looked up at the exotic low white-walled building, with pillared entrance, green roof and window-boxes full of purple-spotted spider orchids. She was exhausted, hot, sticky, and her feet hurt. 'Thank you, Jeremy—I'm grateful. I'll take it from here—if you'll tell me where to report in the morning.'

'Morning? Oh, Ali my dear, you get more than a morning to adjust! Prof isn't expecting you until Friday. The instructions are—just make yourself at home. The Matron will be in touch with you very soon.' He had removed her bag from the boot. Suddenly the pavement was filled with eager, anonymous helpers, and her baggage had been whipped indoors.

A trifle winded, Alanna turned to Jeremy. 'I seem to be taken care of. Thank you for meeting me. I'll be fine now.'

'No problem. Here!' He handed her a small card. 'That's my lodging, and the phone number I don't give to patients. Ring me—I mean it—if you need anything.'

Again, just for a second, she saw his eyes clear, before they clouded over with the responsibilities of his new life. Alanna didn't hesitate. 'I won't need anything. Thank you, Jeremy.'

They stood on the pavement, lit by a thousand neon floodlights all around them. It didn't take much intelligence to realise that the Imperial Hospital was situated in the ultimately fashionable part of Singapore. He said, 'It's been a shock, hasn't it?'

One side of her wanted to pretend that this sort of luxury didn't bother her. But as she looked into his eyes, although they were hooded, and without the teasing spark of merriment she had learned to associate with him, Alanna couldn't pretend with Jeremy. She said, to a background of tropical insects whirring and chirping in amongst the roar of the evening traffic and the tingling of trishaw bells, 'I'm here to do a job, Jeremy, that's all.'

She knew, before he caught her in his arms, that he was going to do it. It was an embrace she didn't need. But almost as though he read her thoughts, he released her from the embrace and stood before her, his arms at his sides. Echoing her thoughts, he murmured, 'We may not see too much of each other, Alanna, but I'm surely glad that you'll be working alongside me as well as with my chief. We need someone like you.'

She looked up at him, and his threat had disappeared. The embrace had meant nothing—just a comradely gesture. He relaxed. 'So I'll see you around?'

'That's exactly it, partner. See you around.'

'Thank you again, Jeremy.'

'It's funny how nice my name sounds in an English accent.' And he turned, opened the door of the limousine, and started the engine, and purred into the stream of traffic.

Professor Kwan Ho Kai was the epitome of Oriental courtesy. 'I am very happy to welcome you, Sister Keith. I am proud of my staff at the Imperial, and your chief gives you an excellent reference. Of course, you must have time to settle down. Shall we say next Monday to start work?'

'I'm quite happy to start whenever you like, Professor,' she told him.

'Well, as you will know, we are pioneering joint replacement here. I've done it for accident surgery, but not for rheumatoid diseases. It's a bold venture for our hospital, but one I feel we must take, and not only take but keep up to date. Mr Masters is my Number One, as you know, and as my other orthopaedic surgeons take over the artificial hips and knees I'm hoping to branch out myself into the small joint replacement field. I believe you are familiar with this?'

'Yes, sir.'

'Then we'll say Monday. The session starts at six-thirty.' He smiled. 'Yes, I do realise it sounds early to you. But we tend to arrange operating lists at the beginning and end of the day—so avoiding the hottest part, when a small siesta is often a good idea. You'll soon get used to our ways.'

Alanna was making for the door when the Professor said casually, 'You—and Mr Masters—were—a little more than colleagues during his time in the United Kingdom?'

Alanna, discomfited, said briefly, 'Did he tell you that, sir?'

'No. But I deduced it. He seemed most anxious that I contact Francis Bates before advertising for theatre staff elsewhere. I assumed there might be some motive for this?'

She said with quiet dignity, 'No, sir, there was nothing more than a professional relationship between us. But we did—enjoy—working together.'

'I'm pleased to hear it, and I hope you enjoy your stay at the Imperial. By the way, should you wish to extend your contract for a further six months, I'll need to know a month before it expires.'

'Yes, sir. But I doubt it.'

The Professor smiled broadly. 'Make no decisions in a hurry, Sister. My city has a way of inspiring affection.' And he opened the door for her with a little bow.

In the nurses' apartments, her little flat had something of a first-class hotel about it, with a maid to clean and wash the clothes, and an excellent cafeteria that seemed to be open all day and night. Alanna soon found her way around—but the girls didn't seem too friendly, or else they were all busy with their own affairs, and she sat alone in the café, and in the common-room, watching the smooth Chinese, Malay and Indian faces of her colleagues, and wondering if there could be anyone else new and strange as she was.

Eventually she made her way to Matron's office in the main hospital block. Matron was efficient, thin and elegantly dressed in a tailored uniform, wearing horn-rimmed glasses on her small Chinese nose. 'I was leaving you to settle in before I sent for you, Sister Keith. Is everything satisfactory? You have been given your rota—and your uniforms?'

'Yes, thank you, Matron.' Alanna was delighted with the cool white cotton of her uniform. She had always thought that dark blue didn't suit her fair hair and honey-coloured eyes.

'There ought to have been information about the hospital and our leisure facilities in your room.' Matron looked at her watch. 'I'll get someone to take you round the hospital, if you like. With a weekend in front of you before you start work, you'll be glad to have somewhere you can relax in.' She rang a bell, and a secretary was asked to show Alanna the 'club'.

Yet more luxury. After taking Alanna round the operating suites, the secretary led her across a quadrangle of lush grass with a fountain shooting diamonds into the blue sky and falling with a tinkling sweetness into a stone bowl where goldfish swam lazily, or basked near the surface of the water. 'This is the staff club. You will be given a pass. All medical staff may use the facilities.' There was a large blue-green swimming pool, four tennis courts, a bowling green, and a cool white badminton hall. Alanna thought with a smile of the dingy hall in Faireholme, with its peeling paint and cheap plastic chairs in the poky little snack bar. This would make Fred and Jo sit up! She thanked the girl for showing her round, and made her way at once to the steward's office, where her name was checked on the staff list and she was issued with her official pass.

Back in the badminton hall, she made enquiries as to times of play, and how to find partners. A cheerful Eurasian girl called Millie offered to give her a game right away, lending her kit and a spare racket. 'We are very competitive here,' Alanna was told. 'We play many other clubs. It is good to find another fan.' And after Alanna had showed her skill, the other girl's welcome was even warmer. 'You will soon be at home here, Alanna. Good players become very popular. Come back at about six with your own kit, and I'll find you a locker. Then maybe we could eat at the club bar.'

Her badminton had done the trick. Feeling that at last she had been accepted, Alanna was promptly back at the club, all worries about the unfriendliness of her colleagues banished by the open welcome of Millie Wong, who was already at the court, chatting in Cantonese to two other girls. 'Ready for doubles, Alanna?' She introduced the others. 'Tonight we have to get on the court early—the men come down, and they try to dominate the women—but we don't let them!'

'Quite right too!' Alanna took up her position, weighing the racket in her hand, happy at last to be part of her new environment, and anxious to show that she could be of some use to the team. 'I'm to receive?'

She bent her knees, eyes on the server. She heard the doors swing open, and allowed herself to peep sideways. The shuttlecock swooped down towards her, but Alanna stood, turned to stone by the appearance of Jeremy Masters and another man, their sports bags over their shoulders.

Millie Wong laughed. 'We must have that again, please! You allow for the sudden appearance of handsome men in the hall!' She turned to Alanna, still smiling. 'That is Mr Masters—Jeremy. He is a very good player, but usually too busy to play in the tournaments. Would you like to meet him?'

'No, thank you.' Alanna turned away, her heart thumping. 'Sorry about that, partner—let's start again, shall we?'

They started the game again, and Alanna excelled herself, whacking the shuttlecock with a passion she would have preferred to expend on Jeremy himself. How foolish of her to allow him to distract her like that. It mustn't happen again. She didn't want to meet Jeremy Masters in any other place but the operating theatre.

They went to the club bar for a wonderful Singapore meal of noodles, prawns and chicken, eaten with chopsticks, which she was determined to get used to as soon as possible. She amused the others by describing, as well as she could, the drab little snack bar where she used to go, the machines that dispensed scorching tasteless coffee, and cardboard cartons of cola or orange juice. 'I think when I go back I'll have to introduce some of your refinements to Faireholme Leisure Club!' she laughed.

'So you aren't homesick Ali?' She realised that Jeremy had overheard her last remark, and looked up, ready with a retort. But the words died in her throat as she saw Jeremy's companion—a wood-nymph of a willowy blonde, dressed in a simple blue silk shift, with a trailing fringed scarf of silver thread round a beautiful slim neck.

Alanna swallowed, and tried to find her voice again. 'Not yet,' she managed to croak, feeling like an enormous peasant woman with her carelessly brushed hair and her simple open-necked cotton sports blouse. That girl must be a model. Who else could walk like that, smile like that, just simply look like that?

Millie looked surprised. 'You know Mr Masters?'

'We were at the same hospital in the UK,' Alanna explained.

'So why don't you want to speak to him?' hissed Millie.

Jeremy's twist of the lips showed that he had overheard that remark. 'May I introduce Camilla Brown? Camilla dear, I want you to meet an old friend from England—Alanna Keith.'

Alanna was forced to stand and greet the lovely Camilla. She didn't offer her greasy hand. 'I'm afraid I'm still an amateur with my chopsticks,' she apologised.

Camilla smiled condescendingly. 'Of course, Alanna—what a pretty name!—it does take quite a time to learn.' Her voice was like a woodland waterfall, cool and elegantly modulated. Alanna managed a quick look at Jeremy. He'd hit the jackpot here. Alanna remembered what Sue had said one day, encouraging her to go out with him. 'Of course he has a string of girlfriends—but one day he has to meet his destiny.' His destiny. . . It looked very much as though Camilla Brown was proving just that.

The couple sat at the bar, drinking champagne and chatting with heads close togther. Alanna tried not to look but stole an occasional glance, her heart hurting with nostalgia, with the knowledge of what might have been. She wished she had brought her panda with her—in memory of the night at the fair, when she and Jeremy had been everything good and happy and close. . . But the panda wouldn't fit into her luggage, and she'd left him in the children's ward at Faireholme, in the hope that his cheerful face and optimistic aura would help some sick children to get better more quickly.

One of the other girls, Amy Low, leaned over the table. 'Alanna, I know it's early days, but how about the hospital team? Maybe start as first reserve? We have a match in ten days' time, and I'm always looking for new talent.'

Lucky in badminton, unlucky in love? 'I'd be glad to, if I'm not on duty,' Alanna told her.

'Wonderful! Thank you. We usually practise three times a week. I'll make sure I leave a message for you in the pigeonhole near your locker.'

She had begun to belong. By the time six-fifteen on Monday morning came, Alanna already knew several other nurses, and felt confident and calm as she made her way up in the elevator to the operating suite. The hospital air-conditioning was quiet and efficient, so that the only moments spent in the hot atmosphere were when she crossed the grass from the nurses' home past the fountain to the main building. And at that time in the morning, the grass was still cool with dew, and the sky translucent and sweet. She wondered, just for a moment, what it was like in Faireholme early on an autumn morning. Frost, maybe, and almost certainly mist. Grey clouds, grey rain and grey stone walls, with faded grass and brown leaves falling from the hospital trees. She looked around her, and gave a little skip of pleasure at the colour and beauty around her. It would be a pleasant six months after all.

'Good morning, Ali.' Jeremy was already dressed in theatre green, as he handed her his mask to tie, and his gloves to hold for him to put on. 'Quite like old times, isn't it?'

'A bit.' Her response was curt.

'Hey, what's the matter? Is it something I've said?'

'No. Sorry.' She just didn't want to talk to him. 'I didn't mean——'

'First day, eh? That's why I thought I'd break the ice by doing the Prof's list this morning. You and I understand each other's way of working.'

'A kind thought, but you needn't have bothered,' she told him.

He beamed innocently, though his tone was slightly sarcastic. 'No need to thank me! Tell me, Alanna, what made you change your mind? I thought you never wanted to leave Faireholme.'

She recalled the look on his face, the day he came and told her he had the job, and asked her to come with him to Singapore. She had refused him very directly, and perhaps she did owe him an explanation. He hadn't mentioned his phone call either. 'Several things changed,' she said lamely.

Jeremy straightened, and turned to stride into the theatre. 'We must talk about it one day soon.' But she could tell by his tone that he didn't really care all that much. How could he, with someone like Camilla Brown around? Taking a deep breath, she walked after him into the room and took up her position at his side. Whatever else was going on in their private lives, she was determined that her work at the Imperial would be her very best.

The patient was having three finger joints replaced

by artificial ones. It was a routine operation for Jeremy
and Alanna, but some of the students had never seen
it done, and the theatre was full of admiring remarks
and interested questions. Jeremy checked the ligature
on the arm before slitting the skin over the first finger,
exposing a twisted arthrosed joint. For a few minutes
the buzz of the saw prevented conversation. As he
switched off the instrument by lifting his foot from the
switch, Jeremy murmured, 'By the way, Ali, how's that
arm I did for Timothy Howarth?'

She was sure he did it on purpose, but it was too
late. It was only a swab that she dropped, but to her it
was like a ton weight falling to the floor, drawing
attention to her clumsiness. Her anger flared. Without
stopping to think who was listening, she turned to
Jeremy and hissed, 'You don't change, do you? Was
that just one of your merry little quips?'

His voice didn't rise. 'Pick it up later, Sister. Pass me
a sterile one.' And he went on carefully dissecting the
joint as though nothing at all had happened. It was left
to Alanna to take herself in hand, pass him a new
swab, and force herself to calm down, and take very
good care to make no more mistakes. She had already
drawn more attention to them both than she ever
meant to. It was going to be harder than she thought
to do this job properly. Six months of this—it's going
to seem like six years! she thought.

But later, just as they always used to, they left the
theatre at the same time, and his smile was apologetic.
'Thanks for coming. I didn't mean to fluster you.'

'I didn't come because of you,' she assured him.

'But you're glad to see me.'

'How do you know?'

He stopped in his tracks, and she had to stop with
him to hear his reply. His voice was at its most melting
as he said, 'We've always been closer than you cared

to admit, you know. Nothing's changed.' And somehow she found it a comforting remark, in spite of
Camilla Brown, and in spite of her careful determination to build a life in the Imperial that didn't include
Jeremy Masters.

CHAPTER SIX

'SISTER KEITH, may I have a word?' The Professor was striding along the corridor as Alanna was going in the opposite direction. She stopped at once as they came close. Professor Kwan Ho Kai was smiling. 'You've been with us a month now, and I wanted to say how pleased I am with your work. My old friend Bates must miss you very much.'

'Thank you, sir,' she smiled.

'You're quite settled in?'

'Yes, thank you.'

'And making friends?'

'I've joined the badminton club,' she told him.

'Excellent, excellent!' His eyes twinkled. 'I'm very grateful for the lectures you've given the nursing staff—most helpful. I must say, it would make us all happy if you'd renew your contract for a little longer. Six months isn't really long enough for you to make up your mind. And I guess the badminton captain would agree with that, not to mention the theatre staff. Will you think about it?'

'Er—yes, I'll think it over.' But so far nothing had happened to make her change her mind. Six months' salary would raise enough money to help her mother out. Tim would by then have got the message that she wanted nothing to do with him. And spring would be returning to Faireholme, a time when she loved it there, to see the snow melt from the distant mountain tops, the yellow pollen on the catkins, and the clean new lambs bleat and skip in the fields around the little town of Faireholme.

Her thoughts were wrested back to the present, and her exotic new surroundings. Amy Low had left her a note. 'Practice on Wednesday, and be there. You're in the second team mixed doubles. Let me know if you can't make it.'

Beaming broadly, Alanna said to herself, 'I certainly can make it!' After only one match sitting on the reserves bench, she was being given the chance of playing for the hospital! It was no mean feat, because the standard was very high in these so-called friendly matches. She had soon found out that Singaporeans had a keen competitive streak, and had little time for losers.

'You're looking pleased with yourself, Alanna. Share the joke?' Jeremy, dressed in starched white coat, his unruly curls brushed back, unnaturally neat, was just coming out of his consulting-room. An Indian colleague with him excused himself swiftly, reminding Alanna of the way his friends in Faireholme used to back off when they saw Jeremy with a female.

She looked up. They hadn't met off duty since the day she had shouted at him in Theatre—something he had commendably made no further comment on. She was getting used to working with him now, and used to the fact that her heart still jerked when she saw him, but it no longer upset her to feel it. 'A very minor matter—I'm playing for the hospital in the next match. There's a practice on Wednesday.'

She expected him to congratulate her at the very least. He played himself—just for recreation, not for the hospital. He knew very well how much she enjoyed her game. But his face was stern. 'I'm sorry, but I can't spare you on Wednesday evening for practice. We've got an important patient coming in for metacarpal and p.i.p. joint replacements. It's a big one, Alanna—I've never done the whole lot before. I'm afraid I'll need you—no one else will do.'

Alanna stood as though he had literally struck her. She breathed in slowly, trying to maintain her cool. He was within his rights, naturally, although her working day was usually over by six, and he would have to pay her substantial overtime. When she spoke, she hoped her resentment didn't show through. 'It would have been—kinder—to let me know earlier. But I'll let Amy know at once.'

'Good. I'll make sure you know when the patient is admitted, and you can come down and see the state of his hands.'

'All right.' She looked up and met his look, the dark blue eyes hard and businesslike. How could this be the same man who had driven his dodgem car with one arm round her, hugging her as he shouted cheerful encouragement to his friend? Oh, how he had changed! 'If there's nothing else——?' She wanted to tell him how much she remembered the old Jeremy, but dared not. There was no point. He had gone, and in his place was a mechanical operating machine.

'No, nothing else at the moment.' He didn't say goodbye, merely turned on his heel and strode off along the soft tiles of the corridor. Alanna watched him until he turned the corner, then looked down again at the little note in her hand, before crumpling it up into a ball in her palm.

Amy Low was at the club that night with Millie. 'That's all right. It happens all the time in hospital. Don't look so glum! That's why we need lots of enthusiasts. I'll put you down for the team anyway, but if anyone plays well at practice, then you'll understand I'll have to give them the place. OK?'

'Of course it's OK,' answered Alanna.

Amy smiled. 'Isn't that your friend over there?' She

was looking over at the pool, and when Alanna turned she saw Jeremy, in brief black bathing trunks, standing on the edge of the pool talking to an Indian beauty in a white bikini. He was no longer the stern taskmaster Alanna had spoken to earlier. He was most attentive to his companion, his hand gently touching her smooth honey-coloured back as they laughed and joked. The girl threw her head back, and her long glossy black hair rippled down to her waist. Amy said, 'You wouldn't think it, would you, but she's a consultant—Dr Lal, a specialist in dermatology.'

'They seem to be very good friends,' said Alanna drily. Where was the lovely Camilla tonight?

Amy looked at her rather sharply. 'Not falling for the handsome surgeon yourself, are you, Alanna?'

'Not me! I've worked with him before, remember? I know his reputation. I've more sense than to fall for such a Romeo. Not my type at all.' So even now he hadn't changed. Still playing the field. Alanna turned away.

Amy Low grinned. She was a tall girl with dark skin and slim long legs, unlike the short, bouncy Millie. 'Not my type either, but I'd give him an hour or two of my time any time he asked me. Some girls envy you, you know—standing at his side every time he operates. What a hunk to stand next to!'

Alanna was still ironic. 'And hand him swabs and retractors? Not very exciting, you know.'

It was Millie who disagreed. 'It's not that—it's the sharing in a cure—you know, both helping to make somebody well. Now that's a good feeling, I'm sure.'

Alanna couldn't deny it. 'You help the surgeons too, with your physiotherapy,' she pointed out.

Millie nodded, and smiled again. 'But we don't get to cuddle up that close!' She stood up. 'Better get going, Amy. See you at the match, then, Alanna, and

I hope you get your chance for the team, in spite of Wednesday's practice being off.'

'Thanks.' Alanna sat still, looking down at her empty fruit juice glass. Thank goodness it was only five more months before she had enough money to help her mother and buy her return ticket to Manchester Airport.

Just then someone called Millie's name, and she turned and waved across the pool. 'It's Chris! You go on, Amy. I'll see you at the courts.' Millie Wong walked over, returning in the company of a young man. 'Alanna, meet my brother Chris. He's staying in Singapore City for a pharmaceutical conference, so I brought him along for a swim.' Chris had a pleasant square face, full lips, and dark almond eyes, that lit up as he shook hands with Alanna. 'Have you brought your bathing things, Alanna?' asked Millie. Alanna nodded. 'Good. Let's have a dip first, and then make Chris take us out on the town!'

'My pleasure. Where would you like to go?' Chris had a low voice, musical and friendly. It was almost impossible not to like him.

When Alanna returned to the pool in her blue two-piece, she noticed that Jeremy and the beautiful Dr Lal were sitting at one of the poolside tables, drinking Singapore Slings from tall glasses, with slices of luscious pineapple on the rim. She was reminded of the day she had looked out of the window and seen him with Emma Forbes, apparently close and intimate, yet suddenly looking up at her, knowing very well she was watching him. Just as on that day, Jeremy suddenly turned and caught Alanna staring at him. A slow, satisfied smile crossed his face as he turned away.

Did he take pleasure in tormenting her? she wondered. Yet Jeremy wasn't to know that he still had the power to disturb her emotions. She acted distantly

towards him. He had asked her to come to Singapore
with him, and she had refused. If only he didn't attract
her glances like a strong magnet, wherever he was in a
room. There was only one cure for that, and that was
to dive in and give the good-looking young Chris Wong
her full attention.

When they had played around like a school of young
porpoises for an hour, and were beginning to feel tired,
Chris beckoned a waiter to bring them lemonade at the
poolside. As they climbed out, dripping, into the hot
tropical night, and sat together, the three of them, at a
table, Jeremy and his Indian beauty were just leaving.
Alanna sat, petrified, knowing full well that Jeremy's
near-naked body was passing within a few inches of the
back of her chair. Please don't speak to me, she prayed.
She didn't want any communication with him, anything
that would remind her of once being close. . . But he
spoke, very politely, very gently, and his voice was still
the warmest, most attractive voice she had ever heard.
'Goodnight, ladies. And I'm sorry about the badminton, but I'm afraid it's out of my hands.'

Millie was carefree. 'No problem, sir. Happens all
the time.'

'Alanna?'

'Not to worry.' Alanna did not meet his look.

'See you tomorrow, then.' And he was gone.

Millie ran off to get changed, already very late for
her practice, leaving Alanna with Chris. The young
man was perceptive. 'That guy a friend of yours? Looks
like a lovers' tiff. Must be about the woman, huh?'

She tried to be light-hearted. 'Not a friend—an ex-
acquaintance. We used to work in the same hospital in
England. It's quite accidental that we both turned up
here at the same time.'

'You sure? That's too much of a coincidence. You
sure he didn't ask for you? Recommend you?'

'I don't think so.' But she wasn't stupid, and she knew it must be obvious it was Jeremy who had asked his Professor to write to Francis Bates and request her to apply for this job. 'He might have told the Prof that I'm experienced with small joint replacement surgery. That's what we're specialising in just now.'

Chris nodded and smiled tactfully. 'I'm sure that's what must have happened.'

'It's annoying really,' she said, standing up ready to go and change. 'Thanks for the drink. I find Jeremy Masters a bit much.'

'Then the sooner we find a restaurant away from here, the better!'

'Why?' And then she saw them, Jeremy and Dr Lal, dressed now, seated in a corner of the bar, a candle flickering between them, and their heads close and intimate. Alanna pretended not to see them as she walked nonchalantly by.

But next morning he was bright-eyed and eager to get on as usual, jolly to all his colleagues, with not a word to Alanna about seeing her last night. They gowned and masked themselves, and operated through a full list, with Jeremy in hearty good humour with the other staff, but with not much to say to Alanna. It was only after the session was over that she noticed him standing casually by the cubicles as she finished off tidying up and putting instruments and equipment away, leaving the theatre spotless. She realised that they were the only two left in the operating suite. She had to pass him to get out. He said, 'You didn't answer me last time. I'm not prying, Ali, but how is Tim Howarth?'

'Tim?' She tried to keep the hardness from her voice. 'All right, I think.'

'I mean, how is his arm? Has he gone back to mountaineering?'

'No.'

'Oh, come on, Alanna!' Suddenly Jeremy's voice became testy. 'I'm only asking a surgical question, for heaven's sake, not propositioning you. I want to know if my operation worked!'

She faced him then, looked into his eyes, and spoke coolly and clinically. 'Then yes, your operation worked. He seems to have full use of the hand and fingers, and he's living a normal life. And there's no need to shout.'

'Then why is he not climbing?'

She said firmly, 'He told me that there's a residual numbness in the hand and that makes him feel he might not be as reliable a member of a climbing team as he used to be. He's happy enough on his own, but he said he wouldn't like to think that someone was depending on him to hold a rope firmly if they were in a tight spot.'

'But there shouldn't be weakness! The nerves were all intact. Is he sure about that?' Jeremy looked anxious. 'If there had been any weakness, it shouldn't have been in the fingers.'

'I'm not altogether sure that he was telling the truth.'

'Go on.' Jeremy was very close, looking seriously at her. 'He wanted your attention?'

'Something like that, possibly.'

She heard Jeremy breathe out a faint sigh of relief. 'Of course! He's sweet on you. Your ex—I should have realised. Playing for pity.' He paused. 'So—that's why you took this job, then?'

'One of the reasons.'

'Good.' He reached out as though he was going to touch her cheek, but drew back his hand before making contact. His voice deepened. 'Do you want to talk about it?'

'I'm sure you won't find it in the least bit interesting.'

'Maybe.' He held the door open for her. 'You're looking flushed, Alanna. If you need to talk, I've always got time, you know that. By the way, that patient I told you about is coming in tonight. Can you meet me in the ward at about eight to take a look at him? Or are you seeing your young man?'

At last she had a chance of getting back at him. To cover her blush, she said coldly, 'Naturally I'll see you at eight. Doesn't business always come first?'

'Quite right—of course it does.' And with a ghost of a smile which he seemed anxious to hide, Jeremy walked off along the airy passage, leaving behind him a scent of man, of Faireholme, of a spring evening at a fair, with mechanical music, with carefree laughter, the smell of candyfloss and a warmth of being together, close and happy.

The girls in the nurses' home were by now much more affable towards Alanna, the sporty types openly admiring her ability to make the hospital team so quickly. She seldom sat alone in the TV lounge now, and knew most of the nurses by sight, if not all yet by name—some of their names being very difficult to remember.

A group was talking about going into town to see a film, and invited Alanna along. 'I'd love to, but I have to meet someone at eight,' she told them.

'Aha! A boyfriend already?'

'Not likely! A consultant surgeon—on business.'

Someone said, 'You work with Jeremy Masters, don't you, Alanna?'

'I do, yes. And with the Professor. And with the senior registrar. And with——'

The girl, a flirtatious type, gave Alanna a playful shove. 'You know who I mean. I'm not interested in the others—only in Jeremy! Can you get me an introduction?'

Alanna shook her head hopelessly. 'That man doesn't need introductions. He went through the entire nurses' home at our previous hospital. He's like a boa-constrictor. My advice to you is to stay away from him.'

'Why, Alanna, want him for yourself?'

She smiled knowingly. 'As it happens, I've said no to him once, and I'd say it again if necessary. I'm allergic to boa-constrictors.

Her friend giggled. 'I'm not—I love a good squeeze now and then!' They all laughed, and in the confusion Alanna was very relieved that they had forgotten the original question, and she didn't have to own up that it was indeed Jeremy Masters she was meeting on the ward at eight.

She wasn't quite sure what to wear. She was off duty, yet seeing a patient. She chose a simple yellow cotton dress with a wide belt that emphasised her slim waist. Again she thought of Faireholme as she dressed, finding it hard to believe that if she had been there, she would have been choosing a tweed skirt and coat, and winter boots.

Jeremy also was not wearing his white coat, but a short-sleeved shirt with a dark red silk tie, and smart grey slacks. He was standing at the door of the ward, chatting to the night sister, a grey-haired Chinese lady whom Alanna had only met a couple of times. 'Sister, this is Alanna Keith, my theatre sister, and a good friend from my previous hospital. You don't mind if I take her along to meet Mr Chou Sen? She's worked with me on this type of problem in England.'

'Of course not, Doctor. But why not bring your assistant surgeon also? Surely he ought to see the case in advance?'

Jeremy smiled, unmoved by her implied criticism.

'He's busy tonight, Sister, but he's coming along first thing in the morning with the anaesthetist.'

'Very well, Doctor.' The sister pointed out the private room, and Jeremy led the way.

As soon as Sister had gone back into her room, he said quietly, 'This is a ticklish situation for me, Alanna. Stand by me whatever you do.'

She sensed his unease. 'Why? What have you done?'

'I'll tell you later. Just now, see what you think of the patient.' And he opened the door and went to the bedside. 'Mr Chou Sen, how are you feeling?'

The wizened little man, in pyjamas so new that they were still creased in straight lines, sat up in bed, and looked rather frightened. He nodded, but said nothing. Jeremy said, 'I've just brought my theatre sister to see your hands. May I?' The patient held out his thin yellow arms, and Alanna was moved by the hands, so twisted and inflamed by arthritis as to be scarcely recognisable as human limbs. Jeremy held the right one very gently, and the man winced at the touch of Jeremy's gentle fingers. He explained to Alanna what he was hoping to do at operation, how he intended to rebuild the entire hand, implanting artificial joints along the knuckles, and in each of the fingers and thumb. 'I've read up all the relevant journals from the States and all Stanley's work in the UK. I only hope the tendons are not too damaged by the disease. The physiotherapy will be very important afterwards. It's the hardest case I've ever tackled, you know.'

After reassuring the little man that all would be well, Jeremy put his hand on Alanna's arm and led her out into the night. 'Come and eat, while I explain it all,' he invited.

'But——'

'Come on, woman! This isn't a pass—it's a business meeting. Don't you recognise the difference?'

'All right. But will you tell me one thing? That little man doesn't look as though he's ever been in a place like the Imperial. Are you sure he can afford this operation? I know the charges at this hospital are astronomical. On top of that, there's the cost of all those implants. How on earth do you know he can afford it all?'

'I just know,' hissed Jeremy in her ear, steering her quickly into the car park and opening the door of his long limousine. 'Get in, please, Al. Quickly!'

She felt pleased at his use of her nickname. Nobody used it here, and it echoed of some of the good times they'd had, a long time ago. She sat quietly, as he drove out of the main city centre and out along the expressway towards the East Coast Highway. It had never been part of her plan to spend time with Jeremy Masters. But somehow she knew this was important, and she had the tact not to ask questions until the time was right.

He drew up after some twenty minutes, at a beach-side restaurant. They could hear the pounding of the South China Sea on the shore, and at a series of stone barbecues along the roadside, families were cooking kebabs and satay, flames leapt and spluttered, and little children laughed and played in the dusk. Jeremy led the way inside the open-sided restaurant, where the tables were lit only by candles, and it was impossible to see people's faces as they ate, talked and laughed together in the intimacy of the shadows.

The owner came up at once, recognising Jeremy. He bore a silver pail in which a bottle of Dom Perignon was already nestling in a bed of crushed ice. 'Good evening, sahib, memsahib.'

Jeremy said, 'Basu, tonight I do you the honour of bringing my best friend to eat here. Alanna, Basu is the best cook in Singapore. The big hotels fight for

THE CALL OF LOVE 93

him—but he prefers to be his own boss. Isn't that
right, Basu?'

The owner laughed delightedly. The badinage was
obviously part of the ritual here. As he levered off the
top of the champagne with a satisfying pop and poured
it into fine tall glasses, he greeted Alanna, '*Namaste*,
Alanna. You do indeed honour me. But why does a
beautiful lady like you spend time with such a rogue?'

Alanna said with quiet determination, 'This is only a
business meeting, Basu.' And the Indian laughed
again, clearly appreciating that Alanna was only
joking. After he had taken Jeremy's order and left
them, she said, 'He didn't believe me, Jeremy.'

He held up his glass. 'A toast. What shall we toast?'

'I think perhaps poor little Mr Chou Sen, and success
to his ordeal.'

Jeremy nodded, his face suddenly serious. 'His—and
mine. It will be an ordeal until I know he can use that
hand again, Alanna.' He sipped the drink, and Alanna
did the same, feeling the effervescence begin to work
in her body, as he refilled the glass. 'You see, he earns
his living as a calligrapher. Now do you see how vital it
is for him?'

She did. 'I also know that calligraphers are poor
men, Jeremy.'

He drank again, then lowered his voice. 'They are.
He is. I'm doing the operation for nothing—and paying
for the implants myself.'

She felt admiration for him then. 'I'd thought you
came here for your own gain—for praise and self-
importance. I thought you'd forgotten what you used
to say about helping the poorer nations. I'm sorry,
Jeremy. I've misjudged you pretty badly on this one.'

'So I'm not quite the playboy you thought? Thanks
for that, Al. But the point is, if I'm found out, there'll
be a lot of trouble. If news of what I've done gets out,

it could cause a lot of hassle for me with the Professor. He runs the Imperial on strictly money-making lines. His staff are employed there because we can ask for large fees. There's no place for altruism. So I'm co-opting you into the secret. You're the only one I can trust not to give me away.'

He was giving her enormous trust. She could easily give him away. Alanna recognised that however she tried to distance herself from him, they did have something of a special relationship, and she secretly exulted at its specialness. She said quietly, 'What about Chou Sen?'

'He's sworn to secrecy. His livelihood was gone anyway. He could scarcely paint a single character without being forced to stop because of the pain. He had to hold his brush with both hands. I knew I could help him, Al—I knew I had to.'

'And after Chou Sen? You can't afford to go round helping lame dogs. Why not just go and work in a Government hospital, and help the poor?'

'Because I need the practice. I'm a very new consult-ant, Alanna, and I can't just go out into the world without getting a lot more experience. So I want to stay at the Imperial at least a year, preferably two. Will you help me?'

She didn't hesitate. He needed her. 'I will, yes. But if I weren't here, who would you ask?'

'I doubt if I'd dare attempt what I'm doing. Now do you see how much this means to me?' He put his hand over hers and looked into her eyes. 'And how much you being here means to me too?'

She nodded, in the candlelight. The combination of the champagne, and his voice at its most mellifluous, and his eyes at their most tender, almost melted her completely. But at the back of her mind were the images of the two beautiful women she had seen him with—the willowy blonde Camilla Brown and the raven-haired, sultry lady doctor. She reminded herself that they were his preferred companions, and that he was only wining and dining little Sister Keith because he wanted something from her. Still, it was a worthy cause, and for once Alanna was willing to be part of his conniving plan. 'Next time, Jeremy, please consult me before you make your plans, not when they're all but complete?' she asked.

'I promise. And thank you, Ali dear. You're a priceless jewel among women.'

A loud sizzling noise preceded Basu with an iron platter on which sliced lamb was still cooking as he ladled it on to their plates. Two other waiters placed hotplates of dhal, rice and vegetables on the table. Alanna picked up her chopsticks and prepared to eat. It was late, and she was hungry. 'It smells quite delicious——'

Another voice drifted into their private world—a woman's voice, cool and sharp as cut glass. 'Why, Jeremy darling—I didn't expect to see you here. And little Sister Keith too! You told me you were working tonight.'

CHAPTER SEVEN

ALANNA was very calm. 'I really have no more time to spare tonight. Please take me back—now.' The elegant and indignant Camilla had been very swiftly removed from the scene, as Jeremy sprang to his feet and ushered her away from their table. Alanna was almost sorry for him as she saw the perplexity on his face in the flickering shadows.

'But you didn't eat anything, Al.' He eased himself into his seat opposite her.

She smiled pityingly. 'Oh, dear! Does it matter so much?'

'Alanna, you know damn well—you know I wouldn't——Oh, lord, Alanna, if only you knew—if only you'd listen!'

Basu, the café owner, reached tactfully across the table and poured champagne into their glasses. 'I hope that the food is satisfactory. I prepare the meat myself, you know, lah.'

Alanna looked up at him, his dark face even more craggy in the flicker of the candle, and recognised the voice of a peacemaker. She looked back at Jeremy and saw the man who was always composed and in charge suddenly at a loss for words. He was a surgeon in a foreign country, and she was well aware of the pressures of his work. She thought of Chou Sen, waiting, petrified, in his brand new pyjamas, for this man opposite her to work the ultimate miracle for him, and give him his right hand back. In an impulsive gesture she put up her hand to touch Basu's arm. 'It looks very good. I'm looking forward to it.' And she picked up her glass and turned back to Jeremy. 'To Chou Sen.'

They ate for a while in silence. There was relief in his face. Alanna had lost her appetite, but she practised using her chopsticks, and found some slight satisfaction in making them work. She found Jeremy's silence disconcerting. 'Is this the first time you haven't been able to make a joke about life, Jeremy?' Her voice was gentle. She didn't want to hurt him any more. She was his theatre sister, his right hand. Until the operation was over, she had no right to do or say anything that might prevent Jeremy from doing his best.

When he didn't reply, she looked up. Then she put her chopsticks down. He was looking at her in the candlelight, his chopsticks poised a few inches above his plate. When he saw her regarding him so gravely, he made an effort at a reply. He started to speak, but his voice wouldn't come. He managed, at last, 'I apologise. I'd like to explain, but,' he shrugged his shoulders, 'you don't seem to want to talk about personal things.'

'No—it wouldn't help. I'm here because I need the money, Jeremy—and I'm going home as soon as I've earned enough for Mum. . .' She hadn't meant him to know that. She said quickly, 'And there's Tim as well. I had to get away from him.'

He looked at her with serious eyes. 'There's a lot more behind those words, Al. . .' But he saw from her face that this was the wrong time for confidences. He drained his champagne glass. 'Would you like coffee?'

They drove back in silence. It wasn't an awkward silence, only one which Alanna felt she ought not to be the first to break. But when Jeremy took a left turn that she didn't recognise, she said, 'This isn't the best way home, you know.'

'I know.' His jaw was firm as he steered the car

through the midnight traffic of Singapore City, with its blaring cabs, gaudy nightclubs, and vulnerable little trishaws, pedalling tourists from trendy hotels. 'We won't be late, I promise.'

Then she heard the music. It wasn't like the fair at Faireholme, but it was mechanical music, accompanied by a high-pitched female Chinese singer, and very soon she saw the lights of a big ferris wheel outlined against the dark velvet of the sky, and heard the typical carefree laughter of men and women out to enjoy themselves. Jeremy parked the car, switched off the engine, and looked across at Alanna. 'Come to the fair?'

She felt the excitement of the music, the cheerful voices, the screams of delighted terror as the Big Dipper swooped down with a roar close by them. The poignancy of the place was not lost on her, with its happy reminders of Faireholme, but she said casually, 'Just for a couple of minutes, then.'

They walked together, and he had to put his arm round her shoulders because of the crush of people. She stole a sideways glance at him. It would be nice to be able to talk to him, to tell of the awful ache inside when she thought of Tim, and the uncertainty of her own ability to be a normal woman ever again. They paused at the sideshows, and laughed at the clowns being plunged into a pool of water if the thrower hit a target. Then they came to a shooting range, and they both stopped. Jeremy's arm tightened around her. 'I won one of those once,' he told her.

They were giant fluffy pandas, in rows behind the Malay showman with a bald head and slanting eyes. She said, 'I had to leave him behind, but he went to a good home—Linacre Children's Ward.'

They were very still then, as though all the bustle of

the fair wasn't anything to do with them. 'You kept it, then?'

She nodded. 'He was sweet. He became quite a friend. The sort of friend who never lets you down.'

Jeremy didn't rise to the bait. 'You took him back on the bus.'

'Yes.'

Quite how she found herself kissing him, she didn't know, but alone in an island of two they stood, in a desperate and clinging embrace that lasted forever. His mouth and tongue explored hers, and she felt his body grow hard and tense against her as they held each other. It had never been like this before. Alanna felt herself unfolding like a flower, accepting his caresses and needing them. His hands moved up and down her back, until they slid themselves inside the undone buttons at her back and clenched against her bare, hot skin. When he let her go, there was nothing to say. She wanted to tell him then—tell him he had proved her a normal woman, that loving a man wasn't the horrid, painful experience that was all she had ever known before. They walked back to the car, and as he drove home he reached out and held her hand with his, so that she wasn't quite sure how he negotiated the bends in the road.

In her flat, she disengaged his arm from her waist. 'I'll make some coffee.' She made her way into the tiny kitchen, her breathing still irregular, and her heart beating loudly. She felt for the buttons on her dress and started to fasten them, feeling herself blushing at what had already happened between them that evening, just because they both felt nostalgic. She yearned to tell Jeremy of the joy his affection had given her that night.

'Don't.' His voice was heavy and low, and his arms crept round her from the back, cupping her breasts

inside her dress and pulling her tight against him.
'Alanna—my lovely——' He turned her round so that
he could kiss her again. But suddenly, frighteningly,
his words set off alarm bells in her memory—they were
words he must have murmured a thousand times to
almost as many women, and words that Tim had used
in some of his more thoughtful moments. . . She
avoided his lips, so that his kiss landed in the region of
her left ear. It didn't deter him, and she had to struggle
with his ardour as well as with her own increasing
desire to turn to him and yield. Afraid now, she knew
she ought to be pushing him away, but with each soft
warm kiss her body felt more languid, and her will to
resist faded as her need to respond grew. Her ears, her
neck, her throat, her shoulders, glowed with fire as he
kissed her, a fire she had never experienced before,
and it threatened to spread out of control as his hands
caressed the parts of her that she had thought—and
had decided—belonged only to her. He was taking
them as his right, and she was giving in the same spirit.
Jeremy Masters was proving to her that she was a
woman after all, as though he knew she needed it to be
proved.

But her joy was shot through with terror, and she
twisted away. The old nightmare of rough hands
assaulting her—her ten-year-old nightmare, of Tim's
throaty grunts, made her break suddenly away from
the sweetness that had turned bitter. She pulled her
underclothes back in place and quickly started button-
ing her dress. 'Not now—oh, not now, Alanna darling,'
he whispered, his eyes half closed, reaching for her,
catching her arm.

She cleared her throat, in an effort to remodulate
her voice to normal, to banish her nightmare. 'I've
been very stupid.'

'How can you say that after——?'

Her voice rose. 'How can *you* take advantage of my good nature? I came out with you for one reason and one reason only—Chou Sen—you were all screwed up about the surgery as well as the money.'

'I'm still screwed up,' he muttered between gritted teeth, shoving portions of his shirt back into the waistband of his close-fitting trousers. 'But now it's a hundred times worse.'

'Don't touch me again. I'm a nurse, I'll help you with hospital matters. If you only wanted a woman, then I'm sure you have plenty of choice in the Imperial, just as you did in Faireholme.'

'I don't want choice. I want Alanna Keith.' Jeremy took a deep breath. 'There's something wrong, isn't there? Look, let's just talk it out. Alanna, tell me what's so very wrong.' His tone was pleading, warm, inviting her to exorcise the demon that was haunting her.

She was too agitated to see it. 'Please go. I think you used me tonight—in fact I know you did. You're too experienced for me, and I made a fool of myself.'

He drew himself up then, and smoothed back his hair with both suntanned hands, so that the muscles in his chest and arms tensed against the thin silk of his shirt. He was a magnificent man. But she had regained her composure now, and with it her determination not to allow Jeremy Masters to add her to his list of notches on his gun. His eyebrows came down over those deep blue eyes, shadowing them in anger. 'You wanted me then. Don't play the innocent with me, Alanna—I'm not the first. You don't get engaged to a man like Tim Howarth without knowing a little bit about the birds and the bees!' He swung round. 'I'll see you tomorrow, then. On a purely business basis. I hope that still stands?'

Alanna swung round to hide the starting tears in her eyes. Her voice faltered. 'I'll be there.'

He paused at the door, and she saw his back tighten for a second. But he didn't turn round, only opened the door, strode through it and closed it behind him with admirable restraint. Alanna walked towards it as though in a trance, turned the key to lock it, and went to bed, flinging her clothes on the floor and leaving them where they lay. But her body ached with unfulfilment, and she lay naked under the thin coverlet for a long time, watching the fan rotate above her, telling herself over and over again that it wouldn't work, that she was fooling herself if she thought she could satisfy someone like Jeremy. His words echoed—I want Alanna Keith. . . Her name had never been said so sweetly.

The telephone woke her, and she reached for it sleepily, after spending too long awake last night. She rubbed her eyes to make sure she hadn't overslept, before picking up the receiver, praying it wasn't Jeremy. But the man's voice that greeted her belonged to Chris Wong, Millie's brother. 'I wanted to catch you before you went to work. Would you like to come out with me at the weekend? I'm sure you'll be busy, but I've heard the new Thai restaurant in Changi is very good.'

Chris had a smooth, gentle, unthreatening voice. She had enjoyed meeting him last time, but did she want any more entanglements just now? 'I believe I'm free, Chris, unless I'm put on standby,' she told him.

'When will you know that?'

'Tonight. But I won't be home till late tonight—my consultant has an evening surgical session. This time tomorrow, maybe?' She couldn't go through life refusing to go out with men. She had to be adult some time. And Chris was nice.

'That's great, Alanna! My lucky day. I'll phone tomorrow, then. Have a nice day.'

She put the phone back in its cradle, her feelings soothed by talking to someone so quiet and gentlemanly. She showered and dressed in a leisurely way, trying to pigeonhole the events of last night as something that happened a long time ago, as nothing to worry over. And she only had to bear seeing Jeremy for six months. She had to work with him while she was here—but soon she would have saved enough money, and would be home again in Faireholme. The time would soon pass.

In the hospital she checked the list on the board. No, she was not listed for standby, and was free to accept Chris's offer. She wondered if Chris had mentioned to his sister that he was inviting Alanna out on Saturday. But when she passed Millie in the corridor, they chatted only of badminton practice. So Millie wasn't coming along, then. Just a twosome. Still, she didn't fear Chris becoming amorous—he was more like a brother with her really. It might do her good to have an uncomplicated date.

She ate supper alone in the café. There were only about eight or nine others eating that evening. She wanted to be composed and ready for the operation this evening. It ought to last about three hours, but she knew the way Jeremy operated, and if he was in the slightest doubt he would pause and take his time, making sure of every detail before carrying on. Outside, the lights were on, the night sky almost hidden by brightly lit skyscrapers. Coloured neon signs flashed, sellers of roasted nuts and charcoal-grilled satay called their wares, and taxis and limousines glided by taking the citizens of this gutsy, vital city to their evening rendezvous.

Then Jeremy Masters came in. He was alone, his

white coat swinging open, and he ordered a coffee. He hadn't seen Alanna, who was seated in a shadowy corner, half hidden by potted plants. She watched him walk over to a table and sit down. He was level-eyed, lost in his own thoughts. She knew his face almost as well as she knew her own—that lean jawline, sensuous mouth, the straight nose and devastating eyes under thick dark brows. She had seen those eyes bright, alert and full of fun so often—what fun they had had, in spite of his wicked reputation! As she watched, she was aware of a deep and languorous longing just to be with him, to be beside him, to touch him, comfort him. It was at that moment that she admitted to herself that she loved him very much.

Her legs felt as leaden as her heart, as she finally rose, walked beside the pool and out of the club, over to the hospital to freshen herself up in the rest-room, before taking the lift up to the operating floor and facing the other staff. Thank goodness they looked to her for guidance and competence. It helped take her mind off her inner problems, to have to cope with the details of setting out the operating theatre, checking that all the sterile packs were in place, the instruments required to hand, the cross-matched blood packs safely stored in the cool cupboard, and all the replacement joints still in the manufacturer's printed pack. 'Do you think Mr Masters can do it—give this man use of his hand again?' asked one of the nurses.

'Yes, I do.' Alanna's voice was firm.

'It seems very strange, putting so much plastic inside a human hand.'

'Look at it in a mechanical way. Mr Masters is removing those moving parts that aren't working very well and replacing them with identical parts that will work—provided the muscles and tendons aren't damaged too.'

'Does he know what damage he'll find?'

Alanna smiled at her junior's keenness. 'Not completely, because on examination the movements are all limited by pain, so it isn't possible to predict.'

'I suppose when he's done more of this type of operation, he'll know what to expect.'

'Yes. Yes, he will.' If he gets the chance. Alanna remembered her promise, to say nothing about Mr Chou Sen's inability to pay for his surgery. He would need more Chou Sens to build up his own knowledge and experience—but if this single operation was a success, it would be a huge boost to his entire career. Alanna went on quietly with her preparations, and murmured a little prayer, both for the patient and for the surgeon.

'Alanna?' A woman's voice. She turned to see Millie Wong, dressed in surgical gown. 'Jeremy thought I'd like to look in on the op. There'll be a complicated management scheme for his hand afterwards, and he said we could discuss it as he operates.'

'Great. Good idea,' Alanna agreed.

'By the way, Chris tells me he's seeing you on Saturday.'

'Yes.' Alanna's heart fell. She wished she hadn't made the date now. Chris complicated things. She wished she hadn't fallen in love with Jeremy. Love was something she would always be a failure at.

Then she heard the voice. 'Sister!' It was peremptory and harsh, and she knew with sinking spirits that he was still annoyed with her.

She turned and went to help him with his mask, gown fastenings and gloves. She could almost hear his heart beating, so close were they, and she felt the heat from his body and the smell of him that sent her senses into overdrive. If only she could tell him now how she felt! She ventured to look up into his eyes as she held the gloves for him. Her glance held his for a few seconds, but she could read nothing in his eyes but concentration on the job in hand. What else did she expect? He was professional to his fingertips in theatre. If only he would lighten the atmosphere, as he usually did, with a few joking remarks to the staff. But Jeremy was silent.

The patient was brought in, already unconscious, and was swiftly intubated. Jeremy turned to Alanna. 'Replacements?'

'All in order, and doubly labelled.'

'Sorry—I didn't need to check with you. You never make a mistake.'

'It's all right.' He didn't need to apologise to her for anything. She knew exactly how he was feeling. But he hadn't lightened the atmosphere yet, so she tried to do it for him. 'But it's the first time you called me Sister. Are first names forbidden tonight?'

There was a pause. She realised the others were listening too, and wondered if she had been too quick to speak. But after a second or two he said, 'I'll never live that one down, will I?' And there was a general murmur as the tension relaxed slightly, and the rest of the team took their places after Jeremy had made his way into the theatre.

After an hour it was evident that everything was going smoothly. The five knuckles were totally in place, and the twisted hand was beginning to take on a more normal look. Jeremy said without looking up, as he incised the skin of the index finger, ready to start on the smaller joints, 'Of course, you all knew it was going to be straightforward, didn't you?'

His assistant, the Indian surgeon named Ahmad,

replied cheerfully, 'Of course, Jeremy. Has anyone ever doubted you?'

Jeremy gave a little laugh, muffled by the mask. 'Only one, as far as I can remember, Ahmad.'

'Well, he was wrong.'

'It was a she, Ahmad.' And again a ripple of laughter went round the theatre. Only Alanna didn't laugh, as she held the retractors steady and kept her eyes on the tiny rotating saw that was teasing away the rotten joint, leaving a space for the replacement to be eased into the healthy bones. Jeremy looked up for a moment. 'Where's Millie? Oh, there you are. Tell me, what do you think the most important procedure will be from the physio point of view?'

'Mobility, sir—I mean Jeremy. Early mobility.'

'Very good. When?'

'As soon as you tell me to.'

There was a chorus of laughter then. 'I wanted you to tell me in how many days,' said Jeremy.

'I know you were. But in this case, you're the boss. I've never seen this operation, and I'll be content for you to supervise my therapy.'

'Very sensible. Don't you think so, Alanna?'

'Yes. Millie is very sensible,' Alanna agreed.

Millie laughed at that. 'And you aren't just saying that because you're going out with my brother, are you, Alanna?'

Jeremy looked up for a fraction of a second, but immediately his eyes were back at his work. Alanna felt his reaction almost physically, although his skilful fingers never paused in their work. Why couldn't Millie have kept quiet about Chris? She said hastily, 'No, not a bit. I just want to get in the hospital team.'

'Naturally.' Jeremy lifted the diseased joint away from the finger, and Alanna handed the retractors to Ahmad as she held out a dish to receive the joint. His

voice was so very normal. But she knew he was taking
in all that Millie had said.

He sutured the fingers himself, taking the same care
with the last stitch as with the first. It was a piece of
work to be proud of, and Alanna knew how relieved
he must be feeling. Now, as he stood up straight and
stretched out his arms and shoulders to relieve the
tension, she wanted to praise him, be happy with him,
explain why she had fended him off, when her only
chance of real happiness lay with him and him alone.

He walked, with those long strides of his, from the
theatre, stripping off the mask and cap as he went.
'Thank you all, very much. I'll treat you to a dinner at
the Dynasty soon.'

Ahmad caught up with him and shook his hand, full
of praise. The two surgeons chatted about the techni-
calities, and the need to get new supplies of smaller
instruments needed in this type of surgery. Ahmad was
asking if there was somewhere in the UK where he
could get the sort of training that would help. Alanna
changed into her street clothes quickly, knowing that
Jeremy nearly always waited for her until she had put
everything away in the theatre, and left it to the
cleaners.

But as she emerged from the operating suite and
made her way to the lift, she found herself alone in the
echoing corridor. The lift swished up for her, empty,
and she rode down, grateful that she wouldn't have to
go through the embarrassment of speaking to Jeremy
again tonight. She stepped from the lift and almost ran
to the lobby. It appeared deserted, with only the
winking neon lights through the glass door making
patterns on the floor and changing the tinkling water in
the small flower-decked fountain alternately red and
yellow and blue. She turned—and bumped hard into
Jeremy, who was just coming down the corridor. He

held her arms for a moment, steadying her, then stood back. 'Oh, there you are,' she said, hoping he didn't notice the pinkness of her cheeks.

He stopped. 'Here I am, all right.' He held out his hand. 'Thank you again for your unstinting support— Sister.' And he let go of her hand, pushed open the doors so that a blast of hot air came into the cool as they went out.

'I've made you very angry, I know.' She ached to explain why, but knew she had chosen the wrong moment.

'It doesn't matter, Alanna,' he said coolly. 'I expect you felt it was your duty to teach me a lesson. You probably thought I might get big-headed and think I could make love to anyone I wanted. I'm glad you got it out of your system.'

They were standing in the street now, in the heat of the night, with the dimmed lights of the hospital lobby behind them. Alanna was glad of the darkness. Her voice was little more than a whisper. 'I didn't want you to think that.'

'What else could I think? For heaven's sake, woman, you've been engaged to be married. You know the facts of life. Why else would you be coy with men, except to put me in my place? You've seen me with other women, and you don't like it, do you, Alanna? How provincial!'

'The facts of life. . .' She repeated the words almost inaudibly. If only he knew how cruel they sounded in that deep, beloved voice! She turned and began to run along the street, tears blinding her so that she didn't know nor care where she was running to. It was late, and there were few people about, or she would doubtless have ended up on the ground. But she ran until she was breathless, then sat on a low wall until after midnight. The air enveloped her in warmth, and the night insects sang for her, but her tears still flowed silently. Her own personal nightmare zoomed into her mind again, and she felt again the searing pain of Tim's hard body, his bruising hands, and animal-like guttural noises. But this time she didn't feel so much fear and loathing. He wasn't a bad man. Maybe he hadn't meant to hurt her. She knew how sorry he was now. Maybe one day the nightmare would be cured. But it was too late now—so very much too late.

CHAPTER EIGHT

BACK in her flat, the phone was ringing. Two o'clock in the morning. Who would call her so late? Maybe someone from England, who didn't realise the times were different. She picked up the receiver. 'Hello?'

'You've been out a long time.'

'Jeremy! Oh, Jeremy——' Her heart was full. He must have rung before, and she hadn't been there. 'Oh, Jeremy——'

'I don't think I said thank you.'

'Oh, but you did, and——'

'Look, I just wanted to say that having you there at the operation gave me confidence. I wanted to tell you that.'

She listened carefully. There was no sign of warmth in his voice. She replied hesitantly, 'That's why I was there—you asked me. I gave up my badminton practice.'

'I know. That's why I thought I ought to thank you again. You've taken your time getting home, I must say. But I saw that your light was still on.'

'Oh,' she said flatly.

'By the way, don't you want to know how Chou Sen is?' he added.

'He'll be all right.' She matched her coolness with his. 'The hand will hurt for a few days, but you've put him right, Jeremy, so he has no worries really. You'll pay his fees, and he'll get his livelihood back.' She could hear her words running away with her, but she had to get them out, now, while she was in the mood, and while she still had the courage. 'And I think he's

111

very lucky to have met someone as—decent and—
honourable as you.'

She heard an intake of breath. Then he said in a
steady tone, 'I can hardly take that at face value. I
know just how many months you've considered me a
Romeo and a lying toad.'

'Yes, but——'

'I'm sorry, Alanna, but the two don't go together.
I'm a lying toad, and for a long time you've made out
that you're too pure a maiden to cross the road to give
me the kiss of life and turn me into a prince. You can't
have changed your entire personality.'

It was Alanna's turn to pause. He didn't believe her,
and his tone was mocking. Chastened but not bowed,
she said, 'Can you tell me which girlfriend's flat you're
phoning from?'

There was a gentle click as he hung up. Or perhaps
the woman he was with had hung up for him. They
were probably having a good laugh at her by now, and
she was incalculably relieved that she must have been
right, and that she hadn't told him the words that were
burning in her head—I love you, Jeremy. It wasn't
nice to be cut off like that—but to be fair, she had
done it to him once.

There was one more operating list with Jeremy before
the weekend. It wouldn't be easy. But Alanna decided
to stick to speaking when she was spoken to, and try to
forget that for a few moments that night she had tried
to make peace. He clearly didn't want to know.

It was Friday afternoon. For some reason Jeremy
was in a very good mood—almost his old self again, as
he joked with the men and paid extravagant compliments to the nurses. He included Alanna in his witti-
cisms, but never spoke to her directly, she noticed. She
looked at the theatre clock, wishing the afternoon at

an end. 'In a hurry, Alanna?' Jeremy had noticed her
glance at the clock. 'Don't worry, we'll soon have this
all stitched up. And if he loves you, the boyfriend will
wait!'

Everyone chuckled obediently except Alanna. Stiffly
she said, 'Life isn't all sex, you know. There are other
people to meet besides boyfriends. Or perhaps you
didn't know that?'

Jeremy was unperturbed. 'Perhaps not—I'm such a
busy man, you see, my dear. A lot of my out-of-hours
education has been neglected.'

The anaesthetist said drily from his position at the
patient's head, 'Better not ask Sister Keith to give you
remedial classes, old man. Not from the sound of her
voice today.'

Coolly Alanna said, 'Not today, nor any day.' And
as Jeremy gestured for the scissors, she slapped them
into his gloved palm.

He snipped the ends of his sutures, handed them
back and said with exaggerated courtesy, 'Thank you
so much, my dear.' It emphasised her ill-manners, and
succeeded in making her ashamed for losing her cool.

The rest of the team were highly amused at the
repartee. It certainly made the afternoon pass, and
Alanna decided just to let it ride, and make her
getaway the moment she could. How glad she was now
that she had arranged to meet Chris Wong. The
weekend wouldn't stretch out like an eternity. She
tidied the theatre briskly, the moment everyone was
out of it, taking a last look around before pushing open
the double doors and making for the changing cubicles.

With a shock, she realised Jeremy was there. 'You
don't happen to have seen the magazine I was carrying
when I came in this afternoon, do you?' he asked
casually. 'Can't find it anywhere.'

She had noticed it. 'The *Journal of Joint and Bone*

Surgery? UK edition? I saw it in your hand. Do you want me to check your office?'

'Not if you're in a hurry.'

'No, not particularly.' She kept her voice calm, wondering why he was holding her back from leaving the hospital. Perhaps on purpose. But perhaps he was just looking for his magazine. She turned with him and went into the small room he used for his X-rays and case-notes when he was operating. The journal was on the windowsill, half hidden by a curtain. 'There it is.'

'Oh, thanks.' He took it from her and turned to go. 'I'm speaking at a meeting tonight, and there are a few points I need to check.' She watched him go. At the lift door he pressed the button, and while he waited for the lift to arrive at the top floor he turned and said, 'By the way, thanks for being a sport during the operation. I was a bit cheeky—but you know me, don't you, Alanna? You coped with it very well. I thought you might have flown off the handle.'

She said, pretending very hard that it didn't matter, 'It isn't my habit to lose my temper during surgery.' But the lift doors had opened, and Jeremy was inside before she had finished her sentence. She watched the closed doors for a while, listening to the lift going down. Maybe he was being deliberately rude. Or maybe he was preoccupied at having to give a talk. She turned and walked thoughtfully into the cubicle to dress, stuffing the theatre clothes down the laundry chute. The end of a week—a week in which Jeremy Masters had reached into her innermost soul—only to decide that he was tired of chasing her, and given up at her very moment of surrender. It proved he never loved anyone for long. He just liked to add pretty women to his list.

She went to the sports club, because it was the logical place to go—and because the food was good, and she felt like a swim before dinner. Millie Wong saw her in the pool, and came over. Alanna swan towards the edge. 'Hi,' she said.

'Alanna, I'm terribly sorry,' said Millie, 'but we won't need you—we've got full teams for Saturday afternoon. I hope you're not disappointed. You've done really well even to get to being reserve after only working here a month or so.'

'It doesn't matter, I didn't really expect a place. But thanks for saying it.'

'I'll give you a bell when the next practice is. Let's hope that the dashing Mr Masters doesn't get in your way again!'

Alanna felt an unaccountable urge to protect him, in spite of everything. 'He couldn't help it. It was his private patient, and that was the only time he could arrange to have the theatre,' she explained.

Millie squatted at the side of the pool and said conspiratorially, 'If you ask me, there's something fishy about that patient. He hardly says a word.'

Alanna was glad of the darkness of the night, to hide her flushed face. Chou Sen had promised to say nothing about himself, but it must be difficult with Millie, who would be giving him physiotherapy every day. 'He's doing all right, isn't he?' she queried.

'Oh, sure, lah. The hand is fine. But he's so— uptight, if you like. And they tell me he never gets any visitors. Funny, isn't it?'

'Not really,' said Alanna casually. 'Lots of people get no visitors.'

'Not if they're as wealthy as Chou Sen. Have you seen the size of his bill? By the time his treatment has finished, he'll cost as much as a three-storey house!'

'I expect he thinks it's worth it, to get the use of his right hand back. How would you feel if you couldn't even write your name?'

'I guess you're right.' Millie stood up.

Alanna called her back. 'Is there a doctors' meeting tonight, do you know?'

'Sure is—a big one. The Singapore Orthopaedic Society. They have a slap-up dinner at the Westin, and then a talk by someone really famous.'

'Famous? You're sure?'

'Of course I'm sure, lah. Why?'

'Oh, nothing. I just overheard something. . .' Alanna waved, and rolled over on to her back, kicking a cloud of spray with her feet. So Jeremy was becoming quite a celebrity. No wonder he had changed towards her, really. He had less time for dalliance now that he had lectures to write and seminars to give. On the other hand—if anyone found out that he was paying Chou Sen's bill, he would lose the status he had immediately. Good surgeons didn't need to pay for their own patients—good surgeons were eagerly sought out, and their favours paid for in exorbitant sums.

She swam for an hour, showered at the club, washed her hair, spent a long time drying it, and then a long time eating her *wanton mee* at a table for one. The floodlit pool was deserted now, the blue waters still as a mirror, and the poolside tables filling up. Her thoughts kept wandering back to Jeremy—the idea of him standing up in front of a roomful of eminent surgeons and explaining his own work was a novel one. Up till now he had been a clever man, a skilful man, a man with a delightful sense of humour and a devastating smile. But famous? Eminent? She couldn't help thinking back to their night at the fair in Faireholme. Dodgems. . . Big Dipper. . .candy floss. Warmth and laughter and closeness. . . Just suppose one day his work became so well known that he received a knighthood? It was possible in a new field of surgery. Sir Jeremy Masters—it had a splendid ring to it. But it placed him very firmly outside Alanna's circle. Perhaps it was just as well things had turned out as they did.

'What are you dreaming about?' It was the registrar, Ahmad. 'I've said hello three times, Alanna.'

'I'm so sorry,' she apologised. 'I guess I must be tired.'

'May I join you? Have a nightcap with me?'

'Thanks, just a little one.'

He beckoned a waiter. 'You must know Jeremy very well,' he remarked. 'He said you worked together in England.'

'We were colleagues, yes.' She smiled. 'But not any more, Ahmad. He's in the jet-set now, I think. And I'm already planning my return trip.'

'You don't like it here?'

'I do like it. But——'

'I think I know. You miss your family.'

'I do feel lonely.' She had rephrased the statement, because it wasn't family she missed, so much as the past. 'I suppose I'm nostalgic for the past. We all have to grow up—and away from childish things.'

'You had a happy childhood, then, Alanna?' asked Ahmad.

'Childhood? Perhaps.' But what she yearned for wasn't childhood, but the carefree joy she had felt, just for a little while, when she and Jeremy had first met. They were like ships sailing on the same ocean, and mooring for a spell in the same place. But Jeremy was a fast clipper, already on the move again, while Alanna was still tugging at her moorings, wondering in which direction she ought to set sail next.

Saturday; and almost before Alanna's eyes were fully open, Jeremy was on the phone. 'It's urgent, Al. Have you possibly got a few minutes? I promise no more, but I must see you.'

Al. He had called her Al, like the old days, and his

voice wasn't flippant or even jokey. 'Do you want to
come round now?' she asked.

'Thanks. Appreciate it.' And he had hung up. She
looked down at her casual cotton kaftan, and decided
not to change. Her hair hung loose round her
shoulders. She had washed it last night, and it shone
with a rather nice corn-coloured glow. But Jeremy
wasn't coming to look at her hair. Whatever it was, it
sounded important. She poured away last night's coffee
and ground some fresh beans. The little flat smelled of
it, with just a trace of the rosewater scent she used, a
light, wholesome perfume that reminded her of
England. She was just hiding some unironed washing
when the bell rang. She slammed the drawer shut and
ran to answer the door.

'Thanks, Alanna——'

'Come in.' It was important for him to realise that
he was no longer welcome to drop in. He had washed
his hands of her, and she had now done the same of
him.

He was wearing an expensive navy polo shirt and
designer jeans, and his hair was dishevelled. Definitely
a man with a wealthy lifestyle, but at present, a man
with a problem. He said more quietly, 'I'm sorry,
Alanna, I really am. It's just that—as you're in on the
secret, I thought you'd help me again. It's about Chou
Sen. Do you mind?' He paused. 'We were friends
once.'

She indicated a chair, and he sank down opposite
her. She brought him coffee, knowing how he liked it
without having to ask. But she spoke in a quiet,
detached tone, with no warmth. 'No, of course I don't
mind if it's important. Is he well?'

'He's fine, thanks. I'm discharging him home on
Monday. But it's the account. I didn't realise that it's
usual for the patients to pay before they leave the front

door. Otherwise, apparently, a lot of them don't pay up at all.'

'And? I don't see the problem.'

'The poor man can't write them a cheque. He hasn't got a bank account, and he doesn't own a credit card.'

Alanna smiled slightly. 'Then I'm surprised they even let him use the bathroom, never mind a bed!'

He met her smile, and raised his eyebrows, beginning to relax a little. 'They believed me when I said he was my patient and that I knew he had the funds. But you see, Alanna, I use the hospital bank, and if I write a cheque, they'll guess what my game is.'

She sipped her coffee. 'When you chose to work at the Imperial, I suppose you didn't know how big a crime it was to operate on a poor man.' Her tone was sarcastic, and not against Jeremy this time, but against the system. 'We may be soft, we Brits, but I'm glad we don't think like that, Jeremy. What can I do to help?'

'Have you got any money?' he asked directly.

She smiled again. 'I'm to pay?'

'No! Oh, Al, help me?' He reached out his hand across her little pine table. He didn't want to touch her. It was only a gesture, but it was a telling one, and it melted her heart a little.

She said, 'I've been saving up because my mother needs money for the house. That's why I came out here. That's why I've done overtime whenever I could. It wasn't your fatal charm that drew me here, believe it or not. But yes, I've got a little money.'

'In what bank?'

'The Hong Kong and Shanghai.'

'Great! Wonderful. Oh, thank goodness for that!'

'I haven't got nearly enough for Chou's account,' she added hastily.

'That doesn't matter. Just give me the cheque. It won't have your name printed on it yet—you haven't been here long enough, and your signature's atrocious, because I've seen it. As long as the finance department get a cheque that doesn't bounce, they'll be happy, and I'll give you cash to put in your bank.'

Alanna reached for her handbag and rifled for the key to her desk. She wrote out the cheque, tore it off and handed it to Jeremy. 'Monday's date. I don't know if this will work, Jeremy, but I hope you'll work out the financial details before you take on your next lame dog!'

He took the little slip of paper and scanned it carefully. 'Alanna, you're a darling! Thank goodness you never learnt to write properly—this signature could be anything. Bless you!'

She looked at him hard. 'I trust you implicitly, of course. I must be some sort of idiot, handing this over on demand. I'll probably end up in prison!'

He stood up then, and came to her. 'I promise you, by Monday it will all be above board. Your bank will have funds, and your mother will have the money that she needs. And I'll be in the clear. This goes into an envelope, and Chou Sen pays it over before he leaves hospital. What can I say? I just don't know where I'd have been without you.'

Alanna felt numb, unable to appreciate his thanks. 'I assume that they don't notice that a man with his hand in plaster can't sign his name?'

He explained. 'They'll assume he wrote the cheque before the operation. And he had bad arthritis—that's why the signature is so obscure.'

He was standing very close to her now, his relief obvious. She turned away suddenly, and twisted the coffee cup in its saucer. 'So you've got what you came for. That's fine. That's what friends are for.'

He breathed in audibly. 'Does it sound so very crude? Alanna, I started this in good faith, helping a man who otherwise wouldn't be helped. Without you, the operation wouldn't have gone so smoothly, and secondly, my name would be mud among the people I most want to make an impact with. I owe you—more than I can say.'

'You owe me the amount on that bill.'

He put his hand in his back pocket and brought out a wallet. 'Go and put that in the bank before midday, and call it quits.' It was a thick wad of notes.

'But——'

'It's OK. Honestly.'

She nodded. 'Right. 'Bye, then.'

'You want me to go?' he asked.

'You can have another cup of coffee, if you like. But I can't see you wanting to stay, after the fool you made of me in Theatre.'

'I always joke—you know I always have. It keeps the atmosphere from getting too heavy.' But he had the grace to look concerned.

Alanna turned and looked up at him as he stood close. With quiet dignity she said, 'Jeremy, if you had no financial worries, would you be here this morning?'

His reply was equally dignified. 'No, I wouldn't dream of troubling you so early.'

'Then there's nothing else to say, really, is there?'

He turned away and walked towards the door. 'Goodbye.'

Something made her speak, say anything so that she didn't have to look at a closed door. 'Did your lecture go well?' she asked.

He turned slowly. 'You really want to know?' And when she nodded, he said, 'It was good. I had something to say, and I told them a lot they didn't know. It did my ego some good. I hope it does the profession some good too.'

She suppressed a smile. 'I'm proud. One day I can

tell people that once I knew a famous surgeon.' She leaned back in the chair, imagining. 'And he once gave me a panda!'

Jeremy reached out impulsively then and pulled her to her feet. There was something he wanted to say, but he held back the words. Instead he said, 'Play your cards right and one day he might give you another.' They stood looking at one another, the screen between them suddenly shattered by memories of the past. He went on, in a low voice, thrillingly intimate, 'And I won't tell a soul that you still owe me seven thousand pounds in gambling debts!'

She remembered the dark plastic of the refectory tables in the Faireholme dining-room, the lingering smell of stale chips and yesterday's custard. And she remembered the table littered with the contents of a box of matches, half and half at first, gradually all being moved into Jeremy's pile. She looked up at him with a lift of an eyebrow. 'You didn't tell me it was so much! Has the exchange rate gone up since you came to Singapore?'

They were both silent. Then Jeremy said, 'They were good days, eh?' He bent to kiss her then. It was a gentle kiss, almost nostalgic, like their mood. But in moments it grew more demanding, and she couldn't forget that she loved this man, that she wanted him, and wanted to tell him so. She put both arms around him, caressing his strong neck with gentle fingers, meshing them in his hair, responding to his kisses with a tender passion, unsure if she were doing the right thing, but sure that whatever they were doing brought a surge of pleasure and delight through her entire body. Her nightmare didn't come back. But the memory of it did, and she knew she couldn't exorcise it until she had told Jeremy.

They heard a sound through their kisses. After

several minutes they heard it again. Slowly Jeremy
drew away, and felt in his back pocket for his bleep.
'I'm on call,' he said.

'Sure.' Alanna hid her disappointment. 'Don't let
me keep you.'

He went to the door and looked back, one hand on
the doorknob. 'Look, when are we going to talk?'

She looked at him sadly. 'Is there any point?'

He shook his head. 'I don't know the answer to that,
Alanna, but something tells me. . .' The bleep buzzed
again harshly, but Jeremy ignored it. 'Alanna, can I
just tell you one thing? I seem to have the reputation
of being some sort of Don Juan.' He looked at her
hard. 'I wonder how that rumour was started here?
I've been far too busy to get involved with women in
Singapore.'

She looked away, knowing she had told the girls he
was a Romeo. 'If I've done wrong, I'm sorry.'

He moved back into the room. 'It doesn't matter.
But, Al, it isn't true. Of course it's true that I've taken
lots of girls out. But I want you to know that I didn't
sleep with most of them. I just like company. Oh, I've
thought myself in love a couple of times—but sex
wasn't uppermost in my mind—not as you accused me
in Theatre of thinking of nothing else.' His voice wasn't
hurt, just his usual quiet deep tone. 'If you don't mind
me saying it, I think you might have more of a problem
in that direction. Do you really think that all men are
just after your body? If you do, Alanna, you're going
to have trouble making any real relationships, you
know.'

The bleep sounded again, and he took a step nearer
the door. Alanna kept her eyes firmly on the floor,
unwilling to let him see the truth in her face. Jeremy
reached out a hand and touched her arm gently. 'If you

ever want to talk, I've given you my phone number. Sorry if I've spoken out of turn.'

'You have,' she said. 'But maybe I deserve it.'

She met his eyes then, and he just nodded, before opening the door and closing it firmly behind him. She went to the window and opened the blinds a little, to watch his perfect figure striding away across the grass. He paused to greet the gardener, and it was clear from the smile on the old man's face that Jeremy had paid him a compliment about the garden. Alanna shook her head sadly. 'I've really messed things up now. Oh why can't I do anything right where Jeremy is concerned?'

CHAPTER NINE

THOUGHTFULLY, Alanna dressed for her date with Chris. Jeremy's unexpected passion of the morning had surprised and touched her, but even before he was out of sight, she told herself that his kisses meant nothing. Yet they had talked more deeply. If only his bleep hadn't summoned him. . . She reminded herself that the reason for Jeremy's visit was to get her cheque, to get him out of trouble. The incidental chat would never have happened if he hadn't wanted her help. He knew—he just knew so very well—how much power his charm and good looks could get him. For a moment she hated herself for responding so eagerly. But she had to admit that her senses had been roused to a peak of physical desire that she found compelling and addictive, and that she had enjoyed every moment in his arms. If he hadn't been summoned back to the hospital, she knew she would never have sent him away. He had even offered to help. . .

She looked at herself sternly in the mirror, and lectured herself. 'You let him down. You gave him an unfair reputation. This is the last time you even think of Jeremy Masters as anything but a colleague. For the rest of your time in Singapore, you make a different life for yourself. Find something else to do! Don't be in when he calls. And treat him as though he were old and crabby and ugly! It's the only way, young woman, not to be hurt any more, and you can do it if you try hard enough!'

It was a happy coincidence that Chris Wong was in town. She had enjoyed their last dinner. Quietly spoken and humorous, Chris had been good company. She chose a fitted silk dress with a full skirt and a rounded neckline that showed off her tan. Fancy being able to wear such pretty clothes, when in Fairholme the nurses would be putting up the Christmas decorations, and hugging their cloaks around them as they crossed the draughty hospital grounds to the nurses' home.

Christmas—her first in a foreign land. She resolved there and then, as she brushed her hair, and reminded herself it needed cutting, to volunteer to work on Christmas Day. After all, her reason for coming here was to save money for her mother. And if she worked during her holidays, she made double the money. That was it—she would use work as a way of forgetting about Jeremy. Fill her days and nights with work, and then there would be no time to allow memories of him to get to her and make her sad.

When Chris turned up at the pool, where they had arranged to meet, he looked handsome and relaxed in pale slacks and an open-necked shirt. He was smiling and his eyes were appreciative of her appearance. 'Millie's over in Sentosa tonight, thank goodness. I always hate running into my sister when I'm out with someone else. Even though I'm very glad it was through her that we met.' The waiter was hovering, and Chris ordered Slings. 'Would you like to see a film, or drive out to Changi? I have my car out at the front.'

'I'm quite happy to go along with what you want to do, Chris,' Alanna told him.

'You won't have seen much of the island, will you, working as hard as you do? Maybe I should drive you to Changi, then. I belong to a club there, and there's a night market to browse round, and some excellent restaurants.' He had a gentle voice, and his English was perfect.

Alanna was relieved to be with someone who played no havoc with her senses. 'It does sound nice—I'd love to. I've never been to a night market.'

'Then let's go.' He stood up while she preceded him from the poolside restaurant, and she didn't allow her eyes to wander around the candlelit tables, in case she saw someone who would upset this rare feeling of peace and harmony.

In the car she asked, 'Last time we met you'd come to Singapore for a conference. Where do you work, Chris?'

He laughed. 'In Singapore! I came to the city for the conference, but my shop is in one of the provinces. We're a very small state. It takes only an hour from one shore to the other, now that the new underground railway is running.'

'Do you do well there?' she asked.

'Oh, yes. The population is healthy, but they always need medication for small infections, and babies always need gripe water and diapers. I do well in my little business. But I'm glad my sister is in central Singapore, because I do love to come and see the bright lights from time to time.' He glanced sideways at her. 'You don't care for the bright lights, do you, Alanna? You're here to work, and as soon as you've finished your contract, you'll go back to your home?'

Alanna agreed. 'I must seem very uninteresting. But yes, you're quite right. I'm here to do a job. That's not to say I'm not very grateful to have some good friends.'

'I hope that includes me,' he said quietly.

'Of course. Though I'm not very lively, I'm afraid.'

Chris took his hand from the wheel for a second to put on hers. 'You're a very pretty girl. But life hasn't always been exciting enough for you. It shows.'

'Does it really?' She tried not to let her thoughts go back to Jeremy at that remark. Jeremy had once said almost the very same thing. But now he knew her better.

'The trouble is,' he went on, 'you're always preoccupied with your work. You should try to get out more.'

'I like my work—and I like the pay too. That's why I came.'

Chris smiled. They were driving into a sparsely populated neighbourhood, and the tower blocks were spaced farther apart, interspersed with silhouetted palm trees and dimly lit village bazaars. 'But work isn't your only interest, surely? I've never met a really pretty girl who had no other hobbies but work. Only narrow-minded spinsters think like that.'

His calm, gentle voice sounded slightly menacing, his words reminiscent of Tim Howarth's first advances. . . Alanna said quickly, 'I've had a very exhausting week, and I don't want to talk about surgery any more just now. But I have plenty of other interests. For instance, I'm a great believer in fitness.'

'Great idea—all the rage just now in Singapore! How do you find that chief of yours? He seems a nice enough fellow.'

The sudden question bothered her. 'I don't want to talk about Jeremy Masters either.' Her voice was suddenly determined, and Chris nodded with an inner understanding as he signalled another left turn.

They had been driving for about half an hour, listening to chirpy Malay music on the car radio, when he turned into a small township. There were some tall brightly lit tower blocks even here, but also along the sides of the road wooden and tin shacks, where wizened brown men sat over rickety tables and drank Japanese beer and ate savoury noodles. Little Oriental-eyed children played in the lush green grass and undergrowth beside the roads, and small crackly radios blared their Malay and Chinese music. 'This is Changi,' said Chris. 'I came the country way, because the main roads are so big and impersonal. I wanted you to see some of the old Singapore.'

'It's fascinating. There seem to be no closing hours,' Alanna remarked.

'Not out here. If the bazaar keeper is at home, then he will sell to you.' Long bunches of green bananas hung from the wooden frames of the huts, green jackfruits and coconuts, and mounds of prickly red rambutans. 'But when—if—we make it to the street market tonight, you'll see capitalism at its most picturesque. Then you must learn to bargain!' They turned into a main road, lined with more sophisticated shops and restaurants. 'You see how the old and modern live side by side? In this town lives the richest man in Singapore. Not in your city penthouse, but in a quiet backwater, guarded only by papaya and palm oil trees, not by bodyguards and fierce dogs. Though he does own an Alsatian or two—as pets!' Chris smiled.

Suddenly Alanna saw water through trees. The rays of the moon made a silver splash that made her blink. 'Is that a river?' she queried.

'No, it's the Johore Straits—across there is Malaysia. Can you see those little lights flickering? That's one of the islands between Singapore and Malaysia. We'll be seeing more of that in a moment.'

And then Chris was parking the car in a well paved car park, and in front of them stood a neat log building, surrounded by floodlit gardens. The sound of splashing reminded Alanna that swimming pools were a standard feature in this fascinating country, and very welcome, in the sultry heat of the night. 'This is my club,' said Chris simply. 'If you like to eat here?'

'Oh, yes. It's lovely.' They entered the building—for a moment feeling the welcome cool of the air-conditioning, before being led out to a wooden balcony

that actually overhung the river. Beneath them the
waves lapped and splashed on smooth pale sand, and
all around them dramatic palm trees towered into the
starlit sky. Chris ordered a meal, while Alanna only
stared in wonder at the beauty all around them. She
was reminded of the song, 'If my friends could see me
now!' But in the middle of this breathtaking beauty,
she thought only of Jeremy. While she couldn't get him
out of her mind, was he thinking of anyone but himself,
his career, his future in Singapore?

'Before you decide that it's paradise, Alanna, rub
some of this on your arms and legs! The mosquitoes
love it here too. The club does its best with insect-
repellent burners, but I'd hate your evening to be
spoilt.' Chris handed her a rub-on stick. 'The ladies'
room is over there.' He grinned. 'Now you see why
you should always take a pharmacist with you when
you go to the beach at night!'

Alanna did as she was told, covering all the bare
parts of her skin with insect repellent in the plush rest-
room. It masked the scent of her perfume, but she
decided that Chris must know best. She washed her
hands and went back to the table, where an ancient
Chinese waiter was just lighting a scented candle before
placing their plates of delicious fish and vegetables
before them. 'This kurau was caught in the bay only an
hour ago,' he told them proudly.

There was soft music coming from an inner room,
separated by a simple Chinese screen, and after they
had eaten, they joined other couples on a small mahog-
any dance floor. Alanna was glad she had worn her
best dress, as she noticed some of the expensive outfits
on other women. Chris held her firmly in his arms, and
she began to feel warmly content. She had never had a
boyfriend who liked dancing. She realised, with some
surprise, that her body wasn't used to being in a man's

embrace, especially for a long time, and at such closeness and with such compulsive rhythms. It was a languid and interesting experience. The last person to have his arms around her had been Jeremy—and his embraces had been compelling in their intensity, in the inner emotions of passionate response they evoked in her own body.

'What are you thinking, Alanna?' Chris's soft lips were close to her ear.

She lowered her eyes, embarrassed suddenly. Surely it was very bad form to think of another man's body when in the arms of one's companion? She stuttered a little over her answer. 'It's just—such a nice change for me.'

'I could dance all night with you. Do you really want to see the night market? Or shall we save that for the next time?' He brushed her cheek with his lips, and she felt a *frisson* of apprehension. 'You don't have to work tomorrow, do you? Surely you're allowed a full weekend off?'

Her apprehension grew. Chris Wong was a gentleman, but she realised their very proximity had aroused him. Very softly, very gradually, he was drawing her body closer to his as they danced, so that their limbs moved in synchronisation. It was time to stop, and to stop quickly. She said the first thing that came into her head. 'What time is it?'

'Eleven.'

'Oh, Chris, I must get back. It's too late—I'm very tired. I told you I'd had a hard week. It takes so long to get back to the city. We ought to go now. I'm—I'm sorry——'

The moon was very bright, an orange ball behind the fronded palm leaves, as he led her out on to the balcony again. There was a welcome breeze rustling in the trees, and the water swished and swirled on the shore beneath them. Chris's voice was tender. 'You could stay at my place—it isn't far.'

He was a nice enough person, she knew that, and it would do no harm to stay with him. She felt very naïve. Something fierce and scared inside made her shake her head vigorously. 'I want to get back—I have things to do tomorrow. Please, Chris?'

The journey back was almost in silence. When the lights of the commercial centre skyscrapers began to shimmer in the distance, he said, 'Money never sleeps, you see?'

She had been watching the east coast highway, remembering when Jeremy had brought her to Basu's restaurant, and Camilla Brown had turned up at their table to ruin their evening. With a guilty start, she said, 'I'm sorry—I haven't been a good companion, Chris. I didn't mean to be so—tired. And boring. . .'

'You weren't. I'm sorry too. I—said the wrong things. Will you come out with me again? I'd like to make it up to you.'

What could she say? Millie Wong was one of her friends. 'Sure—in a while, when I get some more time off.' She knew she sounded reluctant, and tried to be more positive. 'It's been a wonderful evening. I'll always remember it.'

'Me too. But Singapore has lots of surprises. I'll be happy to show you some more one day soon.' His tone was polite, but she sensed it had grown cool.

They drove into the centre of the bright city, throbbing with life as though the night was still young. Casinos and hotels were bursting with evening-dressed patrons, and the sellers of roasted nuts, curry puffs and satay were surrounded by eager customers, as their savoury smells filled the neon-bright streets. With relief Alanna recognised the curved green-tiled roof of the

Imperial Hospital. As they paused at a traffic jam, she said, 'I can walk from here, Chris.'

'Oh, but——'

'It's only across those gardens.'

'I do know where it is.' A touch of his frustration showed through the veneer of good manners. But as the traffic didn't move, he said, 'I suppose it makes sense. If you're sure you'll be all right.'

'Oh, yes. Thank you, Chris, for a lovely time.' And she opened her door and gave him a broad artificial smile before closing the car door behind her and slipping away among the late-night crowds of happy people.

She lay awake for a long while, contrasting in her mind her bodily reactions of that day. Towards Jeremy she had felt magnetised, almost helpless to control her own response to his actions. With Chris, however much she liked him and liked being with him, there had been no physical chemistry and no threat. She hoped fervently that she hadn't annoyed him too much, after the wonderful evening he had given her. Most of it had been lovely. She wondered, as she finally felt her eyelids grow heavy, if Millie would come to hear from Chris of her brush-off, and if it would make any difference to their personal friendship.

She was woken by the telephone ringing. Rubbing her eyes, she realised it was still dark, and she fumbled for the light switch. 'Hello?' What sort of joke was this, ringing before dawn?

'Alanna, is that you?' Jeremy's voice, agitated and upset.

'Yes, of course it is. What on earth's the matter?' She was fully awake in a second.

'There's been a terrible accident—I've got to operate at once. Could you help me, Al, or are you too tired?

I've got to try and save someone's leg—a car crash. Can you help me, please? I could only think of you.'

'It's all right, Jeremy—it's all right.' She found herself speaking as she would to a child. 'I was tired two minutes ago, but not any more. I'll be over. Trust me.' She threw off the thin coverlet from her naked body and pulled on thin jeans and a T-shirt, not bothering with underclothes. Only remembering to take her door key, she closed the door as gently as she could, not wishing to disturb the entire apartment block, and made her way in sandalled feet to the hospital. The air was sweet and warm, with a gentle dew on the grass, and a red glow just beginning in the eastern sky.

A crushed leg—it could be a long operation. Automatically going over in her head what equipment she would need, she hardly remembered going up in the lift, only arriving at theatre, and pulling the curtains modestly as she changed into theatre gown and trousers. It was Sunday. In one strange way she was glad to be working. It stopped her having to think what to do today. Her day was mapped out for her—after this big operation so early in the day, she would be sleepy, and probably spend the rest of the day in bed. She pulled her cap on over her unbrushed hair, tucking the ends inside, and made her way quickly to the theatre that was being made ready, its lights bright against the dark dawn outside the windows.

Then she saw Jeremy. Already gowned, he was standing by the trolley on which lay the still form of the patient. She walked over to him, seeing anxiety in his eyes. 'What time do you want to start?' she asked immediately.

'Alanna, thank goodness! We'll go right ahead now. Ahmad, are you there? Tell Jow we're ready for anaesthesia!' He bent and whispered something to the pale figure on the trolley. It was a woman, slim and young. A strand of pale gold hair escaped from her operation cap, and her eyes were closed. There was a livid bruise on her left cheek, and another on her left arm. It was Camilla Brown.

Alanna felt a cold chill squeeze at her heart. She had been jealous of this lovely girl—but she obviously mattered to Jeremy, and she was badly injured. They had to do their best, or Jeremy would never forgive himself. Alanna turned methodically to her instruments, and arranged everything for instant and immediate convenience. Jeremy came and stood beside her, holding his hands out for his sterile gloves to be pulled on. Alanna didn't look up as she performed this task for him. There was no need for any verbal communication between them. They both knew that he hadn't mentioned Camilla's name deliberately. She sensed his muttered requests before he had even finished them, drawing back the cover and revealing the twisted and broken left leg, once so elegant and perfect, now unrecognisable under its pathetic mixture of blood and iodine. She handed swab after swab, knowing that he would want to do everything himself, even the simple tasks, for the woman he almost certainly loved.

When the wound was clean, he said to no one in particular, 'We'll need a replacement patella.'

Ahmad said, 'The knee should heal up without one. The main joint is stable enough.'

Jeremy paused, his gloved hands tinged with blood, and looked across at his assistant. 'She was a dancer,' he said shortly.

Ahmad nodded his understanding. 'I'm sorry—I'm so sorry. But she—won't dance again, Jeremy, so why the patella?'

Jeremy's voice was tense at his assistant's stupidity. 'She's twenty-one, Ahmad. She's beautiful. How do

you think she'd feel if we cure her leg, but leave it
looking nothing like the right one?'

'Sure,' Ahmad agreed.

'I hope——' Jeremy was turning to look at Alanna.
She reached for the correct plastic wrapping, and took
out the artificial joint. 'Thanks, Al.' He matched it
against the right knee for size. 'Thanks.' There was still
tension in his voice, but as he worked, and the bones
were set, the tendons replaced and sutured, his
shoulders appeared less stooped, and his voice relaxed.
'That's all I can do.' He looked down at the unconscious girl and said softly, 'I'll explain it all when you
wake up, Camilla. But what else is there to say?'

Alanna had the finest sutures ready. She knew the
scars would look ugly at first. But she also knew
Jeremy's skill, and his patience, even for people he
didn't know. Surely, for this woman, he would draw
the edges of the skin together so that within the year
the scars would be scarcely visible.

When the last knot was tied, Jeremy signalled with a
lift of an eyebrow to Jow, who quietly administered the
correct drug to reverse the paralysis, and withdrew the
tube. 'Ventilate? BP is OK.'

'For a little while. It will help to get the gas out of
her system more quickly.' Jeremy dragged the mask
down, but didn't bother removing any other theatre
clothes, as the trolley was wheeled out of the theatre
towards Recovery, where Camilla was connected to
the oxygen supply, and a drip inserted in her right arm.
Very gently, though she was still unconscious, Jeremy
fitted a drainage tube to the wound and placed the
bottle for it to drain beside her bed. 'Where's Sister?'
he asked.

'Here, Jeremy.' It was the sister whom Alanna had
met when she was taken to see Chou Sen. Curt and
unsmiling she was, but she knew her job, and Jeremy

finally surrendered his patient to her care. She said, gently for her, 'Go to bed now, young man. You haven't slept a wink all night, and the sun's well up.'

'You're right, of course.' He could hardly keep his eyes open. 'But you will let me know of any change whatever?'

'You know I will.'

The anaesthetist came up, already changed. 'And I'll be here, Jeremy. Go to bed, old fellow. You've done the hard part.'

Alanna decided she wasn't wanted any more. She didn't want to be thanked—she knew he was grateful to everyone who had helped him. She slipped quietly back to the changing cubicle and stripped off her gown and trousers. She had forgotten she had ignored under-clothes in the sudden emergency, and stood naked in the cubicle. A long cool shower, a cup of strong tea, and a nap. Poor Jeremy—he had seemed unable to believe this could happen to someone he loved. . . Alanna stretched her naked arms, reaching up for her clothes that she had thrown loosely on a hook.

She heard her curtain being pulled aside. Then before she had time to protest or cry out, she heard Jeremy's voice. 'Hell! Sorry. I wasn't thinking——' and then his voice changed. 'It's you, Al. . .' For a few seconds they stood facing one another. His half-closed eyes, his tired brain, were beginning to take in the fact that she wore nothing at all. She saw him look down, then gradually up from her bare brown feet and legs to her body, where Singapore's sun had hardly tanned her skin, as she had usually swum at night. His eyes had reached her face, her tousled hair, her expression of embarrassed concern. 'I didn't mean—this to happen. Oh, Al——' and he gathered her against him, stroking her hair as her head lay against his shoulder. 'Oh, Ali love!'

She heard voices, and panicked. The sight of them both in a cubicle together was bad enough. But without clothes. . . 'For heaven's sake, Jeremy, get yourself dressed. Someone's coming!'

'Right.' He edged away, asleep on his feet, and with great relief Alanna pulled her curtain and dragged on her clothes with little attention to whether they were inside out or not. She reached home without meeting anyone, and locked the door firmly before turning on the shower and washing off her body the traces of iodine, the smell of antiseptic from his gown, the feel of his arms around her. He would probably remember nothing of this when he had slept properly. He was sleepwalking when it happened. But she would remember. She would remember that after he had been through a dreadful trauma, he had spoken to her with relief and affection. Even in his sleep he had been glad and comforted to see her. She scrubbed her damp hair with a towel, and thought that in all their history of working together, perhaps this had been the most genuine thank-you she had ever had. Even though his distress for his girlfriend was deep, yet his obvious need for Alanna, both as a nurse and as a friend, wasn't lost on her; and she glowed, as she flung herself on the bed to sleep, with more than just the abrasion of her towel.

It was dark when she woke—almost seven in the evening. Her first act was to telephone Recovery. Camilla was off her ventilator, and awake and alert. Good. Jeremy would be happy now. Alanna sighed involuntarily. Then she dressed in a simple shift and crossed the grounds to the poolside bar for a lonely plate of *nasih limak*. Not for the first time, she recalled that night at Faireholme when Jeremy had actually asked her to go with him to Singapore. When she had refused, his face had tightened and become aloof, and he had said, 'Well, I tried.' What would have happened if she had said yes? What a pity it was too late now. Far, far too late. . .

CHAPTER TEN

ALANNA found, when she reported to Theatre the following week, that she had been listed to work with the Professor instead of with Jeremy. At first she resented her schedules being altered. Then she began to realise, with a little grin of embarrassment, that it was probably all for the best. Suppose Jeremy did have a hazy memory of what happened? Alanna hadn't forgotten the sensation. Her warm skin against his. . . It was the certain cure for her nightmare, she knew. But Jeremy cared for Camilla, and his caresses that night were out of an almost unconscious gratitude to someone he treated only as a friend.

Professor Kwan Ho Kai welcomed the change. 'I have not seen enough of you, Sister Keith. I wanted to ask you how different is the way we work here, from the methods my old friend Francis Bates uses in his operations.'

'I'll try and tell you as we go along, sir. But the difference in the two hospitals is so enormous that it hardly seems fair to compare them.'

The Prof nodded, and turned to look at her as she stood at his side. He was doing a simple carpal tunnel release of the nerves, and he had time to chat. 'Ah, yes—the money angle. Francis gets all the patients he needs without looking for them. It's easy to gain experience when you have a waiting list. Here, because our system is mainly private, and I am proud to say I advertise in only the best periodicals, there is a shortage of the cases I would most like to learn about.'

'But you were in Britain for some years, sir.'

'Indeed I was—and I learned a lot too. But what about the latest technology, eh? I'm afraid I shall soon have to go to visit my old friend in Faireholme and see all the most up-to-date ideas. I have a friend in Ohio too.'

His SHO said, surprised, 'You mean it, sir? You're taking a study leave tour?'

'I am indeed—the UK and the States. One must keep up with—who is it in England that one must keep up with, Sister Keith?'

'I think you mean the Joneses, sir,' smiled Alanna.

'Joneses?' The SHO was puzzled. 'Is he famous? I haven't read anything in the journals by a Joneses.'

'Explain, Sister Keith!' The Prof thought the whole joke highly amusing, and Alanna's efforts to explain it even more so.

'Who will be in charge when you go, Professor?'

'Mr Masters, naturally.'

'Naturally.' The SHO didn't seem to think it out of order for such a young man to take the part of the leading surgeon.

'But I think I'll leave the financial side to Ahmad,' said the Professor with a twinkle. 'He's a bit more used to the way I work in that field!'

Alanna remained quiet. Jeremy as head of a prestigious hospital seemed a far cry from the young tearaway Romeo she had first met. Yet it was a natural progression, knowing his talent, his skill and his obvious care for his patients. She counted in her head. Her time at the Imperial was more than half gone. She would soon be back in England, leaving Jeremy and his beautiful Camilla to make their place together in the sun. She would leave him to glory in his success, and fly back to spring at home. It would seem a rather empty little home without Jeremy.

There was some early Christmas mail from England

waiting for her—some cards from the girls in
Fireholme, an air letter with Tim's writing on the
front. And a letter from her mother that seemed very
thin. Alanna tore open the envelope. Mum's writing
was always bad—like her daughter's—but this was
almost unreadable. A single sheet. 'Auntie Mabel was
taken ill last week. She was dead when the ambulance
came—her heart, they said. It was a shock to me, as
you'll realise, but I'm grateful that she died peacefully
and quickly.'

And then a telling paragraph. 'My dear Alanna,
there's no need to cut short your contract, as you'll be
home in the spring. The funeral was quiet but well
attended, and I have you to thank for that, dear. What
a difference it made to Mabel's last months, to be out
of that damp bungalow! We both loved our lovely new
warm flat so very much, and even though I have it to
myself now, we made lots of good friends in these
apartments, and I'm never lonely. Thank you for
making it possible. Have a happy time at Christmas,
Alanna, and it would be nice if you could telephone
me, as you suggested. We'll be having a special lunch
at Clayton Court—we've all collected the money
towards a top caterer to do our turkey, and Mr Gray,
my neighbour in the next flat, as an ex-wine merchant,
is in charge of that side of it, and he's quite a card, and
he gets it with discount.'

Alanna smiled sadly. It sounded just like Mum, the
way she talked. Still, she wasn't lonely. It had been
well worth it to give them the money when they needed
it, and to come out to work here for six months, even
though she hadn't survived it without some damage to
her heart. Still smiling, and grateful that her mother
sounded so comfortable, she slit open Tim's letter.

It started off in stiffly conventional words, hoping
that she was well, and getting on all right in her 'alien'

surroundings. But when Tim started to describe his own feelings, it became very clear that he was still cherishing the hope that she would go back to Faireholme, and to a new relationship. 'My dear Alanna, I can't tell you how much I'm looking forward to seeing you again—I recall how I called you my pretty, and no doubt now you have a lovely tan on those delicious legs.

'I'm thinking of spending Christmas with some old college friends of mine, but then I'll be back at the Leisure Centre—no longer living with Fred and Jo, but in my own little cottage, in Green Lane, just off the square—I'm sure you know it. I'm looking forward to showing it off to you. Sue thinks you'll like it.'

She folded the letter absently. She didn't like the way he wrote about her—it brought back uncomfortable and unhappy memories. Would it be sensible to go back to the very conditions she had come here to escape? Professor Kwan Ho Kai was asking her to renew her contract, and for the first time she began to think it might be a good idea. But then she thought of having to work with Jeremy, and she knew that would be difficult. She put her Christmas cards on the bookshelf—it was strange having no mantelpiece, being in a country where there was no need for a fire. Then she put her letters in her desk drawer and locked it. She would postpone her decision about the contract until the very last moment. But the spectre of Tim now loomed over her memories of Faireholme, and made it much less attractive to her.

She put her desk key back in her bag, and rubbed at an irritation on her wrist. Mosquito bite, probably. She looked at it, then stared. There was a group of red bites, and two of them already looked infected. She couldn't work in an operating theatre like this. She must have been bitten last Saturday, in the restaurant

where Chris Wong took her. She telephoned the
Professor's secretary and explained her predicament. 'I
don't think he would want me to work under these
circumstances,' she said.

The secretary agreed. 'Dr Lal specialises in this sort
of thing, Alanna. I'll ask her to see you first thing in
the morning at her clinic.'

'Is that necessary? If I just keep it covered for a day
or two——'

'It's easy to tell you aren't used to the tropics,
Alanna! The bites themselves might not cause too
much trouble, but they can make you very ill. It's
important to have a blood test right away. Will six-
thirty in the morning suit you?'

'Of course.'

Alanna had only seen the lovely Dr Lal a couple of
times, and both of those times she had been laughing
and close with Jeremy—the way Alanna had used to
be when they were at Faireholme, the way they'd been
when gossip had circulated that Alanna Keith was
Jeremy's latest scalp. She presented herself at the clinic
in good time in the morning, but the doctor was already
there. 'Do come in, Sister Keith. Let me see your arm.'
She was dressed in a white coat over a slim-fitting skirt
and blouse that showed her perfect figure and legs. Her
long black hair had been hanging on her shoulders, but
she swiftly bound it up with both hands and secured it
with a single pin before rinsing her hands and putting
on a pair of surgical gloves.

Alanna presented her inflamed wrist, watching Dr
Lal's beautiful face as she did so—such long silky
eyelashes, large limpid brown eyes, full sensuous lips.
No wonder Jeremy had been attracted! Perhaps, if
Camilla hadn't had that accident, he might have con-
tinued dating them both.

'When did this happen?' Dr Lal's abrupt question brought Alanna sharply back to the matter in hand.

'Saturday night.'

'Where?'

'Changi beach.'

The doctor looked disdainful. 'You didn't wear repellent? On a beach at night? That was foolish, Sister.'

'I did wear repellent, Doctor. You can see that the bites are confined to the one spot, although the rest of my arms and legs were bare. I must have washed it off in that spot when I washed my hands.'

'Mm.' Dr Lal appeared still to consider Alanna a fool. 'Well, you seem to have limited the infection. I'll give you some antihistamine to keep on it, and just take a blood sample to test for parasites. You feel well in yourself, do you?'

'Yes, I do.'

'Good.' The lovely Indian fixed a needle to a largish syringe, and retracted it, before taking off the sterile cover and pressing Alanna's arm to raise a vein in her inner elbow. Alanna watched the dark red blood fill the syringe. Dr Lal called to a nurse, who took the sample straight to the laboratory. 'I'll let you know when the results are ready.'

Alanna found herself footloose and temporarily unemployed, with the rest of the day in front of her. She looked down ruefully at the swathe of bandage. What a nuisance, after she had resolved to spend all her time working to keep her mind off other, more painful things. Still, it was her left wrist. She could perhaps still practise badminton with her right hand.

To her surprise and embarrassment, Millie Wong was at the courts. 'My morning off,' she explained, with a cheerful wave. 'Want a game?'

'I'd love one.' Alanna wondered if Chris had told

his sister about Saturday night and Alanna's rather
brusque brush-off. Millie certainly didn't act any differ-
ently towards her. She changed quickly, and came back
to the court. 'Ready, Millie,' she smiled.

'Your day off too, is it?' Millie stood up and picked
up her racket.

Alanna held up her left arm. 'Off sick—mosquito
bites.'

'Ah. That must have been Saturday.'

Alanna's heart sank. 'Chris told you?'

'Oh, yes. He was glowing with happiness—said
you'd had a marvellous time.'

'He did?'

Millie smiled, and sat down again on one of the seats
at the side of the court, beckoning Alanna to sit next
to her. 'Chris was very impressed. Remember he's an
Eastern man, even though he's modern. He thinks
you're very sweet and modest and respectable—better
than some Eastern girls, he said. He said the club
wasn't good enough for you, and he's planning on
taking you to one of the best hotels in town next time.'

'I didn't think—there'd be a next time,' said Alanna
faintly.

'Didn't you enjoy the date, then?' Millie sounded
disappointed.

Alanna had to pretend. 'It was magical, seeing some
of the older houses, and the way the people live. The
beach was beautiful too, and Chris is—very good
company.'

'That's all right then, lah. Let's have that game.'

'I'd love to.' With relief that they were still friends,
Alanna put all her energy into playing a good game. It
was a relief to get back on the court, doing something
she was good at, and she scored point after point
against Millie, who in the past had seemed better than

Alanna. After the game, Alanna thanked her pro-
fusely. 'I did enjoy myself,' she told her.

'I was very impressed!' Another voice came from the
back of the court, and they turned to see Amy Low,
the captain, leaning nonchalantly against the post, long
legs relaxed, and an expression of interest on her dark
face. 'You were damn good, Alanna. If you're
interested, there's a place in the first team for you for
the next match.'

'I'm interested,' smiled Alanna.

'And if you play like that, it's a permanent place.'

'Thanks. I'll do my best.'

Millie congratulated her. 'You deserve it. Look at
you—I haven't even made you sweat!'

'That's because of the air-conditioning,' replied
Alanna modestly. But she was proud of her fitness,
none the less, and after showering and changing the
girls walked back to the hospital together. 'Though I
don't know why I've come. I'm not allowed to work
until the results of my blood test are through, and the
infection has cleared.'

Millie said, after Amy had left them, 'I hear Jeremy
did a marvellous job on our little blonde's leg.'

'Camilla—yes. But apparently she won't dance
again.'

'I don't expect she minds.' Millie was scathing. 'She
wasn't all that good. They say she only got her place in
the company because she slept with the producer. Now
she has a perfectly good excuse for retiring and queen-
ing it as though she'd really been a star.'

'You know her, then?' queried Alanna.

'She was at my old school. Rich palm-oil plantation
daddy, mother ran off with an even richer Indian polo-
player—maharajah or something—you know the type.
In fact, I think Jeremy's anxiety was caused by what

Daddy would say more than genuine care for the girl. But that's my opinion.' Millie looked at her sideways.

'I can't say that I do know the type. There weren't many maharajahs in my part of England,' said Alanna with a smile. Was Millie trying to tell her something?

'I'm going up to the ward now. Want to come along and see some of my patients?'

'Please.' Anything to pass the time. And it would be interesting to see how patients were progressing after surgery. 'They're usually still unconscious when I see them.'

'Mr Chou Sen made a spectacular recovery,' said Millie. 'I've never seen a man so pleased with himself. He kept looking at his hand and bending the fingers. Hadn't been able to do that for years, apparently. And he handed over his cheque at the desk on his way out, with the biggest grin I've ever seen from a man who's just given away fifteen thousand dollars.'

'Yes, Jeremy did mention that he was pleased with your work.' Alanna hoped she wasn't blushing, that the guilty secret of Chou Sen's cheque would remain a secret.

Millie's voice lowered as they came to another door. 'This is Camilla's room. She's still in plaster, of course, but I'm supposed to make sure it's comfortable, and that she can wiggle her toes. Want to meet her?'

'I don't think she likes me,' Alanna prevaricated.

'She jolly well ought to, knowing that you helped Jeremy at her operation. Come one, let's see if she knows how to be grateful!'

'All right.' Alanna was curious herself to find out just what sort of woman Jeremy had got himself tangled up with.

Millie tapped on the door and went in. 'Good afternoon, Camilla. I've got Sister Keith with me today. She was Theatre Sister at your operation, you know.'

Camilla was lolling on her satin pillows, her fair hair spread out artistically. Maybe she was expecting Jeremy, thought Alanna, with uncharacteristic irony. The pose was certainly more artificial than comfortable. 'Hello, Millie. Come to sympathise with me again? I still can't believe this could have happened to me.' Camilla turned to Alanna, and it was clear from the change in the expression on her china doll face that she recognised Alanna, and wasn't too pleased to see her. 'You're Alanna Keith?' Her voice went hoarse for a moment, and she cleared her throat. 'I didn't realise you were so pretty——' She stopped. 'I'm most awfully grateful to you, you know. I have been told how splendid you were at short notice.'

'That's OK. It's a great feeling when a limb can be saved,' Alanna told her.

'Saved!' said Camilla, with a theatrical sigh. 'Saved for what, though?'

Millie was matter-of-fact. 'Saved for walking on and looking good in a short shirt, Camilla. Lots of women would give anything to have legs like yours.'

'You think so?' Still theatrical, Camilla turned to Alanna. 'I'm so scared that one leg will be thinner than the other.'

Millie answered again. 'Of course it will, until I've got the muscles working again. That's my job, Camilla, and I guarantee you'll walk out of here like a fashion model—OK, lah? Now let's see those toes of yours.'

Each toe was wiggled in turn, and pronounced excellent. 'Now I've got an interesting case in the next room, Alanna—a man who——'

Camilla interrupted, 'Do you mind awfully if Sister Keith stays and talks to me for a few minutes, Millie? I'm so bored, lying here with nothing to do.'

'Sure. Catch up with you later, Alanna.' Millie went to the door. Hidden by a silk screen, she gave Alanna a huge wink, before closing the door behind her. Alanna turned to Camilla.

'You know what I'm going to talk about, don't you, Alanna?'

Alanna was immediately on the defensive. Rich this young woman might be, but she would regret it if she tried to intimidate Alanna Keith. 'It might be about the impolite way you ruined an evening of mine a few weeks ago at Basu's restaurant?'

Camilla looked down momentarily, long lashes brushing porcelain-pink cheeks. 'No, but I'm sorry about that. I was shocked, seeing Jerry with someone else. I honestly thought we were going out together, you see, and he did look most awfully interested in you.'

'He did?' Alanna tried to keep the delight from her voice. 'Well, anyway, there's nothing between us, except business. Never has been. Satisfied now?'

'Honestly? You do surprise me. He's always talking about you, you see.'

'You're imagining it,' Alanna told her. 'He probably mentioned me once, because we used to work at the same hospital in England.'

'You've worked with Jerry before? That seems very suspicious to me, both turning up at the same hospital here. And you still say there's nothing between you?'

Alanna's voice had an edge to it now. 'Theatre sisters work with surgeons, Camilla—you must have noticed that. It's essential to work well together, and when we work well together we get a certain professional satis-faction from the relationship that has nothing at all to do with the fact that one happens to be of a different sex from one's colleague.'

'That's very well put, Alanna.' Camilla's tone was too sweet, suddenly.

'So was there anything else you wanted to know?'

'Yes, please—I was wondering if you had any idea who the naked female was who dragged Jerry into a cubicle after my operation and tried to seduce him?' Camilla's words suddenly dripped acid.

Hold on to yourself, Alanna! Don't make any sign, or she'll know it was you. She's bluffing. There was nobody in that department at the time. Nobody who could have identified anyone. Alanna swallowed, and said in as normal a voice as possible, 'I really can't believe anyone would report such an unlikely thing.'

'You know nothing about it?'

'Of course not.'

'Then how did such a rumour get about?'

'No idea.'

'Well, it was only one orderly, actually, the woman who scrubs the floor after the surgeons have finished. But she's quite sure what she saw.' Camilla was eyeing her openly now, and her blue eyes were watching keenly for any sign of weakening. 'The thing is, Alanna dear, you were the only female at that operation—I enquired.'

'The thing is, Camilla, that it was four o'clock in the morning, most of the staff had been up all night, and medical people just don't have the stamina for that sort of thing in that sort of situation. Is that clear?'

The doorknob was turned, and Alanna stood back, glad of the interruption. But when Jeremy came in, looking neat and handsome, his white coat starched and his hair well brushed, she was lost for words for a moment. If only she knew how much he remembered of that morning embrace, his very thorough appraisal of her, those sweet and tender words he had spoken. But they had not spoken together since that day, and

Alanna decided that now was a good time to make a
stage exit. But Jeremy barred the way. Camilla purred,
'Jerry darling, you've come to see me at last! I've been
waiting all day.'

He looked from one girl to the other. 'You—came
to visit, Ali?'

'Not really. I'm just seeing a few patients with Millie.
I'd better go and find her.'

'Just a——' But Alanna slipped past him and headed
for the corridor, pretty sure that even though he
wanted to ask questions, he would never let Camilla
see him rush after her. She caught up with Millie, and
explained that she had seen enough patients for one
day.

Millie came to the door with her. 'Why the rush?
Was Camilla awful? She can be very nasty if she wants.'

'I know.' Alanna tried to smile. 'Tell you about it
some day.' And she made a quick getaway, taking the
back corridor and walking all round the lovely gardens
to get back to her room, so that no one would see her.

She was glad to see that her bites were a lot less
inflamed when she re-dressed her own wrist that night.
But it would be better not to swim, so she walked along
to the club for her meal that night dressed in an
ordinary cotton skirt and top. She really must take this
opportunity while she was off work to go and get her
hair cut—especially as she would be playing badminton
in a couple of weeks. It had never been so long before,
and she pushed it impatiently back from her face as she
found a small table in the shadows. The pool was
floodlit, as usual, and tiny sparkling lights hung from
the palm trees. She had got used to the lovely comforting warmth in the evenings, and she ordered a drink,
and sat back peacefully to watch the swimmers.

From the corner of her eye she noticed two men
enter the poolside area. She didn't turn to look at first,

but something—some inner telegraph, perhaps—made her turn her head casually. Then she turned back again very quickly, shaking her hair down, suddenly very glad it was long, and could hide her face from Jeremy Masters and Chris Wong, sitting down together and ordering beer.

The two men in her life. Chris thought she was a moral and modest young woman—while Jeremy had probably been told by Camilla that Alanna had tried to take advantage of him while he was too tired to protest. What on earth ought she to do? And what if they wanted to talk to her? She felt her face growing very hot, and suddenly the pool seemed to go blurry, and the lights merge into one another. . .

She regained consciousness very slowly. Her first feeling was of relief, because she was in a quiet, cool place, and there were no threatening circumstances. She could hear her fan swinging slowly on the ceiling. But then she began to realise that she couldn't have come here by herself, so who. . .?

Gradually Jeremy's face came into focus. 'Feeling better? You passed out. We thought we ought to bring you home to bed—I found the key in your pocket. I've sent for Dr Lal. She told me you're attending her clinic.' Gradually a second face came into focus too— Chris Wong's. Alanna closed her eyes and wished she had never left Faireholme. Chris's closeness, that had so upset her, brought back her nightmare—the tight throat, the revulsion. . .and she felt herself beginning to feel sick.

Jeremy's voice was gentle in her ear. 'Tell me Ali, love? What's making you so upset?'

She closed her eyes tightly, squeezing tears between the lashes. 'Ask—Chris to go.' Her voice was so low that she didn't know if it was audible.

CHAPTER ELEVEN

ENSCONCED in a comfortable white hospital bed, Alanna didn't sleep well that night. She knew she wasn't ill. But when Dr Lal came to see her, and she saw Jeremy still hovering in the background, she decided to take medical advice and spend a night under observation. After all, those mosquitoes might have given her something nasty. The results of the blood tests weren't yet through. She would have to meet Jeremy again—maybe the whole story of her own personal nightmare would have to be told—but just for tonight she was grateful for the quiet and the privacy.

Dr Lal was the first visitor to her hospital bed next morning. Alanna confessed, 'I feel like a fraud, Doctor. I only had a little faint—I'm really quite well now.'

The glamorous doctor was wearing a blue fitted dress, and her hair hung like a silk curtain down her back. She looked at Alanna with more than professional interest. 'I realise there's a lot more to this business than meets the eye, Alanna. If I had to guess, I'd say you have the typical symptoms of a crush on Mr Masters.'

Alanna returned her look, seeing in her a deeper and more intelligent adversary than Camilla Brown, but still a woman who had more than half an eye on the handsome surgeon herself. 'I'll be honest with you, Doctor——' she began.

'Call me Shakira.'

'Thank you—Shakira, then. I must be one of quite an army of women in this hospital who think a lot of

Jeremy. But it isn't anything to lose sleep about, honestly. I just had a hard game of badminton yesterday, and—there was more than one person at the pool last night that I didn't want to meet.'

'So Jeremy wasn't the cause of your attack?'

'No.'

Shakira smiled, and came closer to take the thin bandage from Alanna's arm. 'Then shall I allow you to get up and go home? These bites are healed, and your blood scan is negative. I would say just stay off work one more day, then start your usual schedules again.'

'Thank you. I'll really be glad to,' Alanna told her.

'I hope things turn out between you and—this other person.' Shakira smiled again. She's glad, thought Alanna suddenly—she's glad that she's eliminated me from the list of rivals for Jeremy! She's in love with him herself!

She sat on the bed in her thin cotton nightdress for a few moments, in the warm quiet room, with crickets singing outside the window, and hummingbirds darting among the scarlet hibiscus, and counted on her fingers. Christmas now was only two weeks away. After Christmas, she had only two months to go before her contract expired. Thank goodness! Surely she could survive without any further intrusion into the hurtful triangle of Jeremy, Camilla and Shakira Lal! She had now dealt effectively, she hoped, with both women. She would make sure that Jeremy too understood very clearly that Alanna Keith wanted nothing more to do with him on a personal level. It only led to complications.

'From now on you're merely one of the people I work with.' She recited the words aloud, so that when she came face to face with him, it would trip from her lips with no stammering or hesitation.

'I beg your pardon?'

She turned, aghast. He stood in the doorway, and for a moment he was almost the young registrar she used to know again, with twinkles in his eyes, and the look of having to try hard not to burst out laughing. 'Jeremy, I wish you wouldn't appear like some white-coated fairy godmother just when you aren't expected!'

He took a step into the room and closed the door behind him. With more gravity now, he said, 'But you must have expected me. You were taken ill at my feet—surely you don't think I'm such a heartless oaf that I wouldn't call in to see how you are on my way to my clinic.'

Alanna took a deep breath. 'From now on you're merely one of the people I work with.'

'I heard that one already. Have you nothing original to say?' The twinkle was back, but he controlled it manfully.

She felt a bubble of excitement inside, a quiver as a giggle was born, and struggled to get out. It could almost have been Faireholme again for a moment. But then she remembered that Mr Jeremy Masters was shortly to be taking over the total surgical command in this hospital, that he had a wealthy female lined up, as well as a ravishing beauty working with him. And Alanna's giggle melted and threatened to turn into tears. It had been such fun for a short time—such wonderful happiness she had felt whenever they met unexpectedly in the grey corridors back home—happiness like a bursting rose, spreading perfume and beauty and joy.

As though he sensed it, he came quickly to the bed and sat beside her. 'There's something wrong. Tell me about it, Al. It was my fault you came out here, and if there's anything wrong I want to help.'

Very seriously now, she said, 'I want to talk to you

in my own time. But I suppose it's better to get it over now.'

'Yes?'

'Do you—do you remember anything at all about what happened after Camilla's operation?' Her heart was throbbing in her chest so loudly that it masked the shrill chirping of the hummingbirds. 'You were terribly tired,' she added.

He put his warm hand gently beneath her chin, and turned her to face him. It was such a nice place to be, so close to him that she felt his breath on her lips, and smelt his familiar after-shave. Jeremy almost whispered, 'I remember everything that happened. And I wasn't sleepy. I didn't mean to pull at the wrong curtain. But everything else I meant sincerely—and enjoyed very much. I'm sorry if it embarrassed you. I felt very close to you that day—grateful to you as well. It didn't seem wrong to kiss you. If I did wrong, then I apologise. Did I do wrong?'

She shook her head, as he still held her face towards him, his fingers warm and gentle against her skin. 'But Camilla knows,' she told him.

He sat up then, taking his hand away. 'I thought we were alone.'

'An orderly saw us. I told Camilla nothing. Maybe you could do the same, tell her the orderly was mistaken, and then the story would be scotched?'

He nodded. The bleep sounded in his pocket, but he didn't move for a moment. 'I'll do that, Alanna. Tell me—why do you care anyway? The story would die down of its own accord.'

'I don't want any silly stories spoiling your future career, you see. Prof told me you'd be taking over from him shortly. You're going to be someone important and big in this society, Jeremy, right to the top. I know you care for Camilla, and I want you to have every chance of—a good life here.'

He stood up abruptly and went to the door. 'Thanks for that. But I never said I cared for her.' His voice sounded choked. 'In fact——'

'Jeremy?'

He paused but didn't turn round. His shoulders were tense, his hands clenched. 'Yes?'

'There is something else. But I can't tell you now.'

He stood very still, and looked down, kicking away an imaginary speck of dust. His back was still towards her. He said, 'I wish you trusted me enough to tell me.'

There was a long pause, during which Alanna tried to find the words to tell him she did trust him, very much. 'It's just—that I don't think it would do any good to go into details. After all, your future is here, and mine is back in Faireholme, I guess.' Her voice trembled, as she thought of Tim, his bearded face, fanatical eyes, groping hands.

He turned round then, and walked slowly back to her bed. 'I have to say it, Al—I could tell when you fainted. You were scared of Chris Wong—simply and completely terrified. I'm guessing, but it reminded me of the way you looked when Tim Howarth used to bother you.'

Alanna said nothing. She was glad that Jeremy knew. And she recalled his sarcastic words, about knowing about the birds and the bees. . . She whispered, 'Don't let it bother you.'

'Bother me?' He sat down on the bed and looked into her eyes. She was too mesmerised to look away. 'Alanna, I'm the idiot who teased you about the facts of life—got angry with you for pushing me away. It's true, isn't it? You have some terrible fear of being touched—of being made love to?'

She looked down then, unable to meet the blazing

sincerity in his eyes. He went on, his voice comforting
and warm. 'I'm so sorry, my dear—I was cruel and
unfeeling. I was no better than the man who did this to
you in the first place. Did he—rape you, Ali? How old
were you?'

'Seventeen.'

He said nothing for a while, looking towards the
window as though thinking. Then he spoke again, very
quietly. 'As I said, I think I could help you. Would you
let me?'

She took a breath before saying in a very low voice,
'I don't know.'

'Ali, I know you didn't come here because of me. I
know damn well it was because you needed the money.
Only now I realise that you had to get away from
Howarth as well. But primarily, you didn't come
because of my fatal charms. I have to accept that, and
I do. But we do have a kind of special relationship,
don't we? You trusted and helped me over Chou Sen,
and I'll never forget that. You let me kiss you—and
you kissed me in return. I don't want to pressure you
in any way at all, but I think—that being with me from
time to time can maybe exorcise that devil of yours.
Do you see what I mean? No pressure. No promises.
Just friends.'

She was surprised at her own clarity of mind as she
replied, 'You're right. You have been—special to me,
and I admit it. Thanks for saying it.'

'And you want me to help?'

'I think I do, please.'

'You trust me enough?'

'You did say just friends?'

'I did.' He tilted her face towards him, and, seeing
her look of relief that they finally understood one
another, he leaned forward and kissed her full on the
lips. His mouth was warm and moist, and she pressed

towards him, to keep him with her just a few seconds
longer. As he drew away, she saw in his eyes that he
recognised her need of him. It was difficult to admit
her vulnerability, but she knew that there was no one
else she trusted so much. Jeremy let his hand fall to the
bed. 'We'll work it out, you'll see. I'll show you how
sweet it can be to give pleasure and to take it—share
it. . . No strings, I promise. Now stay there and get
some sleep. You can go home this evening. And don't
forget where I live.' He stood up and went to the door.
This time he didn't pause, but left the room and closed
the door gently behind him.

Professor Kwan Ho Kai pinned up the notice of the
hospital dinner-dance where everyone could see it. He
was taking over the Shangri-La Hotel Cascades Suite,
with its real indoor waterfalls and brilliant coloured
lighting, for his staff for a whole day, so that those who
were on duty in the afternoon could attend the evening.
Millie was Alanna's informant that Camilla Brown was
walking with crutches, and had called her dressmaker
into the hospital to design a stunning creation for this
very event. 'And Jeremy hasn't even invited her yet!
So far, it's staff only!'

'He will invite her, though, surely?' queried Alanna.

Millie agreed. 'Well, he's friendly with her old man.
It might be good politics to stay in cahoots with old
man Brown—he can boost anyone's career. Now as for
Chris—he was hoping you might——'

'Invite him as my guest? Couldn't you?'

'Yes, I could, Alanna, but I think it would mean
more, coming from you.'

Alanna grimaced. She didn't want to offend Millie.
'I hope he doesn't read any more into it than just
friends?'

'He hasn't a hope with you, you mean?'

'He's a great guy, Millie, but——'

'I suppose once you're in love, no other guys are a turn-on, lah?'

'I'm not——' But Alanna couldn't lie to Millie. She had been too good a friend. She just smiled a little thinly, and nodded. 'It's—tough when you know it, and there's no hope.'

'I think you and Jeremy are the best of friends. I've seen you together. You read one another's thoughts.' Millie was being encouraging, but failing. 'I'll make sure Chris knows the score.'

'Friends—maybe. I used to think we were like ships that pass each other just once, then go on to find completely different ports to settle in.'

'That's very poetic, you know that, Alanna?'

'I've had a long time to work it out,' Alanna grinned, trying hard to keep her tone cheerful.

'Let's go to my place and try clothes on.' And they left the poolside and went back to Millie's flat. 'You tried to miss this party, didn't you, Alanna, by volunteering to be on duty? You didn't realise that the Prof starts it in the afternoon, so that everyone can go!'

'Don't I know it! Never mind. I don't have to stay long.'

'Long enough to eat something, and dance with the Prof.'

'Dance?' echoed Alanna.

'You're a good dancer—Chris said so.'

Alanna, resigned, looked at Millie, who was standing in her bra and briefs, trying a long royal blue embroidered cheongsam in front of her at the full-length mirror. 'I'd better phone him now, hadn't I?' She reached for the phone and dialled Chris's number. He sounded overjoyed to be invited. Alanna felt like a heel when she put the phone down. 'He can make it,' she said.

Millie was about to fling the cheongsam on the bed when she said impulsively, 'Hey, why don't you try

this? You'd look a million dollars in it. And you could
have your hair up. What do you say?'

'Me, in a dress split up to the thigh?' laughed
Alanna.

'It's traditional. Anyway, you don't mind showing
your legs in a swimming costume. Just try it. You're
about the same size as I am—a bit shorter, but the
cheongsam is short for me anyway.' And Millie showed
Alanna how to fasten the diagonal opening.

'It fits all right,' Alanna agreed.

'It looks great, lah. Right, now tell me which I
should wear!' And they had strewn the entire contents
of Millie's wardrobe around the room before she made
up her mind. 'I wonder what Camilla has chosen? I bet
she won't look as nice as you.'

Alanna wished she wouldn't go on about Camilla.
But there was no getting away from the fact that she
thought she had her hooks into Jeremy Masters, nor
that Jeremy and Camilla's father belonged to the same
club. . . 'Don't pretend. You know she's got a lovely
figure. She'll look stunning.'

'I guess I know. Maybe I'm just jealous too!'

Never was Alanna so relieved that she was working for
the Professor instead of his Number One that week.
The talk over the operating table was all about the
coming party, the lavishness of the food that was always
provided, the number of top bands who were invited
to play for them, and the famous pianist who would
play during the dinner. 'My wife is wearing purple this
year,' admitted the Professor. 'She thinks she looks
like the Empress Josephine. What colour are you
wearing, Alanna? I hope you don't clash, as I want you
to meet her.'

'A sort of blue, I guess—I think it will go with
purple.'

The Professor twinkled at her above his mask. 'That's good news, my dear. Someone told me that you had planned to stay away.'

'Who was that, sir?'

'I'm afraid I can't remember exactly.'

But Alanna had a very strong feeling that Jeremy had asked him to find out if she was coming, so that he could invite Camilla. After their little tête-à-tête, he wouldn't care for the embarrassment of Camilla and Alanna being there at the same time. She said coolly, 'Then you can tell this person—if you remember his name, of course—that I'm going in the evening, so he can go before nine if he wants to avoid me.'

'I'm sure there's no one in this hospital who would want to avoid you, my dear. Just the opposite, in fact.' The Prof sounded as though he meant it, too.

Although not looking forward to the party greatly, Alanna found herself caught up in the spirit of excitement. The girls in the nurses' apartments planned to meet at the poolside bar for a drink together before the hired cars came to take them to the Shangri-La. Alanna showered, powdered and perfumed herself, and wondered what Sue would be doing, back at Faireholme. Whatever happened, and wherever she went in the world, she would never forget the excitement and the glamour of this fantastic city state and its lovely, colourful people.

She wore the cheongsam, with high-heeled gold sandals that matched the embroidery. She began to feel glamorous, a strange feeling to the usually down-to-earth Alanna. She swept her shining hair up into a gold clasp, borrowed from the girl in the next flat, that held the chignon firmly. And she inserted glittering sapphire drop earrings, borrowed from Amy Low, that made her feel like an empress herself. Then she sat at the mirror, and wondered whether she dared wear make-up. It would be silly to wear mascara that might run. Her face was tanned and healthy. Maybe just a hint of blusher, and a bold lipstick to match the striking beauty of the dress.

The comments from the girls confirmed her satisfaction with herself, as she walked slowly, unaccustomed to heels, and unwilling to stride out, as she didn't want too much thigh to show through the gold-edged slits in the skirt.

'It isn't really Alanna, is it, lah?'

'She's much better-looking than I imagined.'

'I prefer English girls with a tan. Alanna makes Camilla Brown look like a pint of milk!'

She reached them at last, and smiled. 'What I want to know is, how much do I owe Millie if I spill anything on this thing!'

Millie laughed. 'Didn't you know? It goes in the washing machine.' She handed Alanna a fruit drink. 'Better not to drink anything stronger. Prof provides wine with the meal, and plenty of it. If you don't watch the waiters, they keep filling your glass.'

'I'll remember.' In all the fuss and excitement, Alanna had almost, just for a few moments, forgotten Jeremy Masters. But she remembered him then, remembered the night when he had taken her to a country pub, and actually suggested that they got married. . . He could have been hers that night. But where would he be now? It had been the right decision, to refuse him. He had been a playboy then, and would be one still, had the pressures of his position given him more free time.

The centre of Singapore was jostling, as always, but the Professor's fleet of cars got through, and were waved into place by uniformed Sikhs with turbans and glittering scimitars, who bowed to the women as they walked, two by two, along the red carpet into the magnificent entrance hall of the hotel. Alanna was quite unused to such admiring looks. 'This must be how film stars feel all the time,' she said to Millie.

'They think you are a film star! You look like one.'

'I feel more like Cinderella—one night out, but a real life of rags.'

'Cinderella got the prince, remember,' laughed Millie.

'I wonder if Chris is here yet.'

'He won't be late. He had a new evening suit made just for tonight.' Millie sounded proud, and Alanna's heart sank.

Inside the glittering hall, trays of drinks were already being offered, and soft music was playing. Millie and Alanna paused, looking round the room for a suitable table, not in too much light. Women in brilliant gowns turned out to be colleagues—radiographers and secretaries and nurses. Men in white dinner jackets were humble housemen, analysts and pathologists. Then Millie said, 'It looks as though Prince Charming is alone, Alanna. Over there—by the piano.'

Alanna stood erect, looking regal, but with a fluttering in her heart. He had come alone. He hadn't seen her yet, but he was clearly looking for someone. 'I've never seen him looking like that,' she whispered, almost to herself. Familiar, yet so far away. An old friend from her past, maybe for the present—yet not for her future. A man as close once as anyone had ever been—yet never to be close again. Her eyes sought his, but though he looked in their direction he made no move.

She turned away, trying not to be disappointed. After all, she had made it very clear that they were to be nothing more than professional colleagues, but she'd thought, after their talk, that he would come to her that night, especially as he was alone. The earrings swung against her neck, reminding her that she was elegant, glamorous, the equal of anyone here tonight. She turned to watch other wonderfully dressed guests arriving, looking for the purple velvet that would signify the arrival of the Professor and his wife. Then she heard a voice behind her, a voice that could only belong to one man. 'Millie, where on earth is she? Don't tell me she chickened out on me!'

And Millie said quietly, 'Alanna.'

She turned round, her heart beating fast. He had sounded quite worried. Jeremy stood there, dressed in impeccable white tuxedo, his tanned face the handsomest she had ever seen, ever loved. His face changed, admiration mingled with relief, as he realised who she was. 'I say. Oh, I say! I didn't recognise you.' He seemed incapable of speech, or of movement.

She didn't know how long they stood there, while the rest of the room vanished. She thought of a million things to say in a single second, but couldn't say them. How she wished she had never spurned him, never teased him, never made it clear that she had no time for Romeos. 'Jeremy.' It wasn't much of a greeting, but it was all she could manage.

At last he took a step near enough to take one of her hands in both his own. His voice was husky and low as he said just to her, 'Well, now you know what the word "stunning" means. Because I'm just knocked out here. Have you ever known me lost for words?'

'No, I can't say I have.'

'I'm—so proud of you, Ali. So proud. I want to stand up on the table and shout to the whole world—this is my girl, and we come from the same place——'

'With a fairground in summer.'

He stopped again, his eyes dark with memories. 'I know things aren't quite as they were in Faireholme—

but maybe you'll dance with me? I'd like the chance, before I get flattened in the rush?'

'I'd like to, Jeremy. But I better warn you I'm not used to these shoes. I'd hate to stab you in the foot with a stiletto heel.'

He smiled, and his eyes lit up as they used to in the old days. Again the rest of the world disappeared, and Alanna felt a great longing to be in his arms. In a moment she would be able to hold him, and she would know by the way he held her if perhaps tonight would be the night they stopped their voyaging in different directions, and came together, even if only for a short while.

Then their brittle world shattered into a million pieces, as she heard Chris Wong's voice. 'I'm terribly sorry, Alanna. I hate myself for not being here to meet you, but I had to go and chat with the Professor's wife, and I dared not leave her until she gave me permission.'

Alanna turned, her evening falling about her feet like a shroud. She had invited him, and there was no way she could leave him so quickly. 'It's all right, Chris. You did the right thing.'

'You're very beautiful tonight. But then you're always beautiful, Alanna. There's a photographer around somewhere. Will you give me permission to have a picture of you with me?'

'If you must.' She turned to see if Jeremy would make a similar request, but with a pain in her heart she saw he had already tactfully left them, and she saw him in the distance, joining in a group of the high-ranking consultants. With them was Shakira Lal, her hair swept up with pearls and white flowers, her gown of black velvet slashed to the waist at the back. 'Now that's stunning,' she muttered to herself, as she turned back to Chris and Millie.

Chris saw where her eyes were drawn. 'Your colleague from England is a very jolly man, Alanna. He knows some very good jokes. He must be fun to work for, I would imagine.'

'Oh, yes—when he's in the mood.'

Chris said gently, 'His girlfriend is arriving. I saw her car—it is a white Rolls-Royce, isn't it?'

Millie nodded and said drily, 'That's one of them.'

Alanna looked at her. 'You knew Camilla was coming?'

'I didn't know for sure. I just know that she's a very spoiled and determined woman. She usually gets what she wants.'

Alanna laughed rather too loudly at the remark. 'I wonder if she gives lessons,' she said. Then, seeing Chris's gentle face look puzzled, she took his arm, crushing her disappointment behind her like a discarded flower. 'I'd love to dance, Chris, if you think you could risk my heels.' And his face glowed, as he led her to the floor and took her proudly in his arms.

CHAPTER TWELVE

THERE had been an unexpected phone call early on Christmas morning. 'Happy Christmas, Alanna. Would you like to come to the Cathedral with me? It's just occurred to me that we might go together. The English service starts at eleven.'

'I'm sorry—I'm afraid I'm on duty in a minute. But—have a very happy Christmas, Jeremy.'

'I ought to have thought of it earlier. Maybe I'll see you later?'

'Maybe.' She didn't want to sound too eager. It was a nice thought—especially as she was feeling particularly homesick. She wondered whether to ask him if he had enjoyed the party—but he had already hung up. Oh, well. Just friends. He wasn't to know that she had left the party before midnight alone, just like Cinderella, her evening turned to rags because he hadn't asked her for a single dance.

She worked until Christmas Day, sunny, bright and sultry, was almost over. There had been three emergency operations, performed by the registrar, and she had been happy enough to assist at all of them. It helped a lot, being bright and helpful to unfortunate people with pain and post-operative problems. In between, she visited the in-patients, chatting to the lonely ones, and entertaining the children who were not already surrounded by adoring family and expensive toys.

She came off duty at eight, and went straight to the flat to telephone her mother. The lines were engaged a few times, but she persisted, and eventually heard the bell ringing in her mother's little flat. It rang for a long time before it was picked up, and a very hearty male voice asked who was speaking. 'Please tell Mrs Keith it's her daughter,' said Alanna.

'Ah, you're the lovely Alanna!' He sounded merry, and she wasn't surprised that her mother was also in the middle of a very happy and giggly luncheon party.

After a little chat, in which she told her mother precisely nothing at all, but Mum didn't notice, she rang off, and after pressing the lever down held the phone in her hand for a few moments, wondering whether to ring Sue Long. The lines would probably be engaged anyway. But it was worth a try. Slowly she dialled the old familiar Faireholme number. Was it still Beryl on the switchboard? She heard the phone ringing its old-fashioned burr. No new-fangled switchboard for Beryl. The call was answered suddenly. 'Faireholme Hospital.'

She would have liked to chat to Beryl, but it was an expensive call, so she just asked for Sue's extension number. 'OK, love. It's Alanna Keith, isn't it? Happy Christmas, pet. I'll just give her a buzz for you. Enjoying the tropics, then, are you?'

'Oh, yes, thanks, Beryl.' Fortunately someone picked up Sue's phone, or Beryl might have gone on all night with the local news, of which she knew as much as anyone.

'Hello?' It was a man's voice. Good old Sue—a boyfriend at last!

'Is that Sue's number?'

There was a pause. Then the man said, 'Alanna?' and she knew who it was immediately.

She tried to control the shake in her voice. 'Yes, Tim. Happy Christmas. Has Beryl put me through to the right number?'

'Oh, yes, it's Sue's all right. I'll call her for you.

She's in the kitchen.' She heard him call. 'There's a
call from abroad for you, Susan.'

Sue sounded flustered. 'But it's lovely to hear from
you! How are you keeping?'

'All right,' said Alanna.

'How's Jeremy?'

'I hardly see him.' Not quite true, but safest.

'Oh, that's a shame. We were all hoping—oh well,
never mind. I bet you're having a smashing time.'

'Yes—smashing,' Alanna agreed.

'Look, Ali, about Tim——' Sue began.

'You don't have to explain anything. Is it serious?'

'I—I think so. I didn't mean to——'

'And you're happy?'

'Yes.' A sincere and emphatic reply.

'Then so am I for you,' said Alanna.

She put the phone down eventually, with a strange,
empty feeling inside. She had spoken to the people
who meant the most to her in England—and found she
didn't really miss them at all, and they most certainly
were getting on very well without her. Suddenly there
seemed to be no good reason to go home, to cold wet
weather, no real friends, and a large drop in salary.
Poor Faireholme, how much I used to love you, she
thought. Yet there you are, getting on with things in
your own way, and Alanna Keith is most definitely
surplus to requirements.

Camilla had looked beautiful at the party—a real
English rose, in swatches of lace and satin and diamonds. No one could see that her leg was still in
plaster—anyway, it was very suitable for the queen of
the evening to sit on a red throne-like chair and receive
her courtiers with a gracious smile. Jeremy had
danced—once with the Professor's wife, once with
Shakira, and once with Millie. Alanna had danced with
Chris, with Ahmad, and with the Professor. And now

she sat, feeling like Cinderella who had forgotten to leave a shoe on the steps. No shoe—and definitely no prince! But it appeared plain that Camilla commanded him, even though Millie Wong kept reminding Alanna that it was Camilla's father whose good books Jeremy really had to keep in.

The telephone rang. Surely Jeremy wouldn't try again—but her first thought was that somebody was being very kind, remembering her on Christmas Day. When she answered it, it was only the hospital. 'Mr Masters wants to see you in his office. Would first thing tomorrow be suitable?'

She was not officially working on Boxing Day, but she had nothing else to do. 'Yes, of course—I'll be there. Does he want me for theatre?'

'No, Sister Keith, it's just a business matter. About his proposed lecture tour, I think.'

'Lecture tour?'

'Oh, not right away. Next year, after the Professor comes back from his trip to the States.'

The Professor was not proposing to be back from his own study trip until the following July. He had confirmed that at the party. So Jeremy Masters was assuming that Alanna would be available then, although her contract was due to expire in March. She wondered if he could be a mind-reader, guessing that after her UK telephone calls that evening she had almost made up her mind to sign on again. After all, she loved the work here, and the weather.

She didn't dress to impress Jeremy next day. She had done that at the party, and although he had shown genuine appreciation he hadn't even asked her for a dance after Chris had showed up. She wore black cotton jeans, a jade-green silky top, flat black pumps. She let her hair fall loosely down her back, giving it a good brushing, but not bothering with make-up. The

THE CALL OF LOVE

morning was bright, but there were billowing grey
clouds threatening to build up into a tropical storm that
afternoon. She crossed the neat grass and brilliant
hibiscus and bougainvillea beds of the hospital grounds,
said good morning to the gardener, who patiently fed
the goldfish in the fountain, brushed up every fallen
petal, every leaf or twig that dared to drop on the
tailored lawns, and turned into the shadows of the
entrance hall.

She looked around her as she entered. Yes, she had
come to a decision. Alone as she felt just now, she
would stay. This place was home now. The porters
greeted her from behind the ornamental fountain in
the foyer, as did the little Malaysian domestic, pushing
a trolley on which were fresh vases of orchids and bird-
of-paradise flowers for the luxuriant corridors. Two
nurses, coming off night duty, stopped and hoped she
had a happy Christmas. She made her way in the lift
towards Jeremy's office. She wouldn't let her feelings
for him spoil her life here. They had reached a certain
warmth of feeling, and nothing more. It was just
something she would come to live with.

His secretary smiled. 'You're prompt, Alanna. He's
only just in himself.'

'I'll wait, then.'

Jeremy appeared at his door. 'No, come on in,
Alanna. I'd like to sort this out today, if you don't
mind.'

She went into his room and he closed the door. He
was wearing smart tailored grey trousers, a white short-
sleeved silk shirt and his plain dark red tie. His face
was grave, his brow slightly furrowed. She had never
seen him quite so preoccupied over paperwork,
although many times he had been under great strain
while in Theatre, which was soon dissipated afterwards
with his famous jokes and good humour. She said

rather sadly, 'This is what you get when you make it to the top, then.'

He looked up, and his face cleared. 'What are you talking about?'

'Your worried look. That worldly-wise air of having the troubles of the world on your shoulders. It comes with the job.' She smiled, teasing gently.

'You're telling me I'm beginning to look my age?' He smiled back, and the worry lines vanished. 'What impertinence! You'd have something to say to me if I said anything like that to you! Now sit down, woman, and listen carefully. I've got to make some decisions here, and make them before Friday.'

'Go ahead.'

'Will you come to Thailand with me in July?'

'I beg your pardon?'

'Operating, Alanna, operating. I'm invited as guest orthopaedic specialist at one of the prestige hospitals in Bangkok. Will you be free to come along? I want someone who can both work in Theatre with me, and also lecture to their nurses on the requirements of specialist orthopaedic nursing.'

She blinked. It sounded high-powered. 'I was just wondering why you thought of me, Jeremy, when you know my contract is only till March,' she said.

His reply was immediate, almost as though it was rehearsed. 'You can't go back to Faireholme. Not after the successes we've had here. Your career is on an upswing, Alanna. Unless it's for personal reasons. . .' He looked at her with a raised eyebrow. 'It would be a step backwards, and you know it.'

She nodded, composed. He might be wondering about Tim Howarth, and she decided that there was no point in hiding anything from Jeremy. He was the nearest thing to a friend she had. 'Yes, I know it. I'd decided to stay on, but I did wonder why you took it for granted.'

'Because I know you very well indeed.' He paused, and looked at her, but didn't smile. 'Because, if I'm honest, I work best with you, and I like you around— you bring out the artist in me.' Then, suddenly there was more than a hint of the old twinkle, but it was soon gone, as he looked back at the sheaf of papers on the desk, and she might have imagined it. 'I don't want to rush you, but it would be a weight off my mind if this could be finalised quickly. I do want to know where I am before the Prof goes away on his American jaunt.' He looked up again. 'Oh, he's going to Faireholme too, you know—operating with Batesy. He'll take any mementoes we want to send to old acquaintances.'

'That's nice,' she said drily. If he was hoping she would rise to the bait and give away her own feelings about Faireholme, he could forget it. But she owed it to him to mention Tim. 'Sue's going out with—Tim. I spoke to them last night. They seem very happy.'

Jeremy picked up a paper. His face didn't change, but the paper rustled as his grip tightened on it. 'Good. This is the form for you to fill in. I'm sorry, but as your chief I have to know your age—there's a space for it here.' His face was completely straight, yet she could have sworn he was laughing at her underneath. The Jeremy she used to know would have been. She took the form from him and scanned it. He said, 'Any problems?'

'No. Shall I sign it now?'

The mask slipped slightly. 'You're a brick, Ali!' Then the mask came down, and he was again the stern employer. 'Yes, go ahead. You can sit here in my chair.' He moved out of the way, and handed her a gold pen to fill in the form.

She filled in her details absently, automatically.

Name, address, age, qualifications, past experience. . .
But her thoughts were elsewhere. This is what it will
be like. Close to him, working for him, yet never dear
to him. Could she do it? Alanna wasn't sure, but she
knew that most things healed with time, so maybe she
would settle for a business relationship rather than
nothing at all. 'It's a long time——'

'Sorry?'

She realised she'd spoken her thoughts aloud. 'A
business life—a career. It's a long commitment.'

She signed her name, and handed him the paper. He
took it and perused it thoughtfully. 'Very long—and
one where a wrong move could be a disaster. That's
why I'm glad you've made this commitment with me. I
think we'll both benefit in the long run.'

She didn't reply for a moment. 'That's it, then?
Anything else?'

He walked round the desk, and sat down again, his
eyes on his work. 'Nothing else, thanks.'

She waited for him to say goodbye, but he appeared
lost in concentration. She turned quietly and walked
out of the room, her feet silent in their rubber-soled
pumps. What did he mean, mentioning her age like
that? It wasn't funny. Why were women's ages always
funny, when men's weren't? In a few years, if he went
on like this, Jeremy Masters would be a plain boring
old businessman. He would have totally lost all that
fun, all that idealism that was such an essential part of
his charm. Then perhaps she would fall out of love at
last, and her life would belong to her again.

The following week she was handed new schedules
by the administrator, and noticed that she was back
with Jeremy. He must have decided that all the embarrassment of their escapade in the cubicle was forgotten
and behind them. When he turned up to operate, she
played her part quietly and efficiently as usual in

theatre. It was a routine session, of simple tendon repairs, a trapped elbow nerve, and a rheumatoid wrist to be fused, with Jeremy speaking little except to ask for what he wanted. Alanna shook her head to herself. Already he's turning, she thought. No joking in Theatre any more, and even a look of reprimand instead of a quip to a nurse who dropped a kidney bowl.

Afterwards she changed quickly, after her usual final look around to make sure all was neat and put away in the theatre. She didn't want to see Jeremy. It was depressing to see the change in him from a vibrant Technicolor personality to a grey man with nothing but schedules and money on his mind.

But he caught the lift just as the doors were closing. 'You're quiet today. Everything all right, Alanna?'

'Fine, thank you. And you? How's Camilla?'

'The leg is well healed. The scar shouldn't be too noticeable.'

'And dancing?'

'She's thinking of going into her father's business.'

'What qualifications has she got for running a business?'

'A great love of money.' Again, a single flicker of the old Jeremy. It didn't sound like a grand passion at that moment, but she knew old Mr Brown was taking Jeremy under his wing. They had reached the ground floor, and said no more to each other. What a sad, grey conversation. What a waste of a fine man, a wonderful sense of humour, and that infectious smile. No sign, either, of what Camilla meant to him as a man.

The next two sessions were very much the same. Thank goodness she had her chance in the badminton team at the weekend. What a great opportunity to whack at the shuttlecock as though it were her very life, and she was whacking the greyness and the annoyances out of it. She had no doubt at all that she would win her match. She had all the frustrations of the week to vent her strength on, and she was looking forward to it.

'I'm putting you on first.' Amy Low lectured the team before the match. 'Alanna, their first woman player looks old, but she's had years of tactical experience, so don't just hit out—watch her intentions before you make your move.'

'I'm ready,' Alanna assured her.

Alanna was in her element, and at her peak of readiness. But when she saw the wiry little Oriental lady on the opposite side of the net she saw a mean streak over there, and a fanatical determination to win. Alanna recalled all the times she had been told in her life that she was a very strong woman in spite of her own slight physical appearance. Jeremy had said it too. She looked across at her opponent, and her eyes said, Alanna Keith is sore with life at the moment, and is going to take it out on you!

Her opponent won the first point with a decisive smash in the opposite corner to where Alanna expected it. She would have to take some knocks, in order to get opportunities to get in some of her own. It was tight— first one and then the other in front. Alanna hardly heard the crowd urging her on. It became a personal battle against the gleaming eyes of the little woman with the muscles like steel cables.

But she never gave up, and she won as an infuriated opponent hit the shuttlecock just too far, and it was called out. A tremendous roar rose from the onlookers, and Alanna was showered with hugs and kisses and praises.

'Very well done, Ali.'

She thought she was imagining it. Jeremy couldn't

possibly be there. But he was—and dressed in whites too. 'What are you doing here?' she wanted to know.

'That's not a very nice welcome!' he grinned. 'I'm your partner in the mixed doubles. So come and rest now. Take it easy—we've got lots of time. Would you like cold fruit juice?' The welcome ice rattled in the two jugs he held. She took a tall glass of cold lemon, as they found a quiet spot outside. 'I've never seen such a fight. You were quite magnificent.'

'I didn't know I'd be playing again,' she confessed.

'And you weren't expecting to play with me?'

'Right!'

His voice was teasing. 'And do you mind playing with me?'

She looked up at his fresh face. It had come alive since the last time she saw him. It was young and lively and very handsome. His eyes shone, and his smile was natural and heart-stopping. 'Jeremy, I don't mind who I play with. But you have a rather worn-out specimen as a partner. I feel sorry for you.'

He moved nearer, not exactly touching, but close enough for their bare thighs to share their warmth. 'And I don't mind either, because I'm not here to win. I'm here to be with someone I like to be with.'

It was a sweet thing to say, but she was conditioned not to let his compliments get to her. She fended him off with a joke. 'That's fightin' talk where I come from, mister! I ain't playin' with a pardner who ain't fightin' to win.'

He held out his hand and she took it. It was only in fun, as they shook hands. Then he said, with a strange and beautiful look in his eyes, 'That's OK, then, pardner, because I think I've already won.'

The atmosphere had changed. Alanna tried to keep up the joke, but it came out slightly breathless. 'I sure hope so.'

Amy Low came outside. 'You two ready? It's almost time for you.'

Jeremy stood up. 'We'll be along, skipper.' He waited for Alanna to stand beside him. 'I'm thoughtless—I should have let you grab a shower and a change of clothes.' He looked contrite. 'I'm not taking this tournament seriously enough.'

'I can change my shirt in two minutes. See you on the court.' It was delightful that he hadn't changed into that grey man of yesterday, that he was still capable of being light-hearted, even with all his awesome responsibilities piling up. Something about him charged up Alanna's feelings and got the adrenalin flowing, so that when the pair of them walked out on to the court for the final, deciding match, her step was as jaunty as his.

They won. Tired as she was, she was also buoyed up by Jeremy's company. He gave her a hug when he scored the winning shot. They shook hands with their opponents. Amy Low and Millie were patting their backs and calling them the new Imperial stars. Jeremy excused himself. 'I'm afraid I must rush,' he said, when Amy asked him to join them later by the pool. 'I've got an important date.'

Alanna might have known. She should be used to such let-downs. She showered, and changed into her old jeans and a loose shirt. Her hair was still damp from the shower, but she combed it back, and stuck her gear in the laundry. They would be waiting for her at the pool, and it would be a sweet moment to be toasted as the new champion. She looked forward to a Singapore Sling, a plate of *wanton mee*, and an early night. What better way to celebrate the imminent New Year? Her new life at the Imperial was starting, and she was surrounded by friends, cheerfulness and opportunity. No time to grieve for what she couldn't have.

She emerged from the shower block, to find her way

blocked by a man—a man in old jeans, a red T-shirt
and sneakers, with unruly curls that had obviously been
washed but not combed afterwards. She looked up into
Jeremy's face, and saw a deep, deep ocean behind
those dark blue eyes. And she saw a smile. 'You're not
going, you know. I've got other ideas.'

'Jeremy, they're waiting for me,' she protested.

'OK, we'll go along later. There's something I want
to show you first. Will you come quietly, or do I have
to pull rank and carry you kicking and screaming over
my shoulder?'

A bubble of a laugh welled up. A bubble of nostalgia, too, as she saw again the man she had loved.
'Well, that does sound quite fun——'

'But you'll come anyway?'

'I'll come anyway.' And she didn't mind at all as he
tucked her hand into the crook of his arm and led her
away by the side exit. 'Where exactly is this thing that
you want to show me?'

'Jump in here, and I'll show you.' He pointed to his
long limousine. 'You're a bit scruffy, but I'll make an
exception this time.'

'I'm scruffy! What about you?' They were just in
time. As Alanna banged the passenger door and fastened her seat-belt, the monsoon that had been threatening all day came down, and in seconds the car was
inches deep in water, and the windows completely
blotted out by drenching rain. They were steamed up
at once, and Jeremy hastily turned on the engine and
the car's air-conditioning. 'Ready?' he asked.

'You're not driving in this?'

'Only a shower. Hold on!' And with his famous grin,
he eased out of the car park and into the slow-moving
blur of lights, rain and exhaust fumes that was the main
road.

'Is your journey really necessary?' asked Alanna.

She was gazing at him, hardly trying to hide her pleasure. The rain beat noisily on the windscreen, and the wheels swished through pools of water, not draining quickly enough down the monsoon drains at the sides of the road.

'Nearly there.' And through the driving rain she saw lights high above them. For a moment she thought it was a skyscraper, but the lights began to move, and she realised it was the Big Wheel. They had arrived at the fairground.

Jeremy parked the car in another puddle. 'Get out, then.'

'I'll get wet,' she protested.

'So will I.'

Surely he didn't mean it? But in the frivolous mood that wrapped around them both, she opened her door, stepped out into the fierce storm, and walked nonchalantly across the car park towards the stalls, that were being buffeted by a playful gale that bent the palm trees double and ripped off their leaves and ripe coconuts, and sent them hurtling along the streets. Within seconds he had caught her up, put his wet arm firmly around her, and guided her inside a sheltered arcade, where soaked pedestrians waited for the monsoon to subside. 'Good girl! Now, we're almost there.' And he led her to a shooting range, where Chinese and Malay youths were trying their skill. Behind the wrinkled brown stallholder was an array of stuffed toys. Including giant pandas. . . Alanna looked up at Jeremy with a large grin, then burst out laughing at his dishevelled hair and shirt clinging to his muscled torso. 'Oh, Jeremy, you never change, do you! And I thought you had. . .'

He shook his head, laughing at her lank streaked hair and putting it back from her face with a gentle touch. 'No. Wait one second.' He found his five dollars,

and took a rifle. He was a good shot—she already
knew that. When he won a prize, she expected him to
be given one of the stuffed toys, but he pointed at
something else. It was a cheap ring, with a very large
piece of glass in imitation of a diamond. The stallholder
handed it to him with a grin.

He turned to Alanna then, holding the ring in his
hand. 'I never change—not with you. But you didn't
believe me, did you, Ali? You thought I was a toad
and would stay one.' He reached for her left hand, and
very gently put the toy ring on her third finger. 'Will
you marry me? And will this do until tomorrow?'

She found that tears filled her eyes, prevented her
seeing or talking. He looked down, and pulled her into
his arms, into a damp and endless embrace. She clung
to him, feeling the strong, beautiful body of the man
who belonged to her and always had. 'Why did you do
it?' she whispered.

'Pretend? It was the only way. You never thought I
could be serious about anyone, did you?'

'I suppose not. But I was beginning to, after we had
that talk. Then you went and ignored me at the party.
I didn't know what to think.'

He drew away and held her shoulders, so that he
could look into her eyes. 'Do you know, Ali, that
you're the only woman in the world who looks ravishing when she's wet through?'

'Better than at the party?'

'That was hard, pretending to take no notice of you,
I have to admit. But I wanted you to want me.' His
voice deepened. 'I want that very much. When you
took me into your confidence, I began to hope. But
until you say it, love, I won't really believe it.'

She clung to him, unwilling to let go. 'Do you think
we'll enjoy going to Thailand?'

He nodded, his eyes warm and smiling and full of

love. 'Of course we will. We're going to enjoy every moment of our lives from now on. It's going to be fun, being with you—I promise. Starting tonight.'

Their arms were tight round each other as they started to walk back towards the car. The rain was just beginning to ease a little, the drumming on the glass roof less thunderous. Tonight. At last the ache deep inside was gone, the longing for the fun of the past replaced with the joy in the present, and glorious optimism about the future. 'Tonight? Why? What's happening tonight?'

His lips were kissing her hair as they walked, and his voice was muffled. 'Tonight? Oh, I thought maybe a little discussion—back at my place? We need to decide a few things—where to be married, where to spend our honeymoon, how we're going to spend New Year's Eve, that sort of thing. I gave you my phone number the moment you arrived in Singapore—and you never rang me once. So tonight you pay the penalty! Is that agreeable to you?'

She smiled up, and there was no need to say how happy she was. 'You know, Jeremy?' she began.

'What, my darling?'

'I didn't want a panda anyway.'

'You didn't?'

'No. You're better-looking, and you haven't got black rings round your eyes.'

The rain had stopped, and a crescent moon was low-slung in the sky. The Singaporeans parted in two on the crowded pavement, past the couple embracing. Some of them smiled. Love was a happy thing.

Very much later, Alanna stood alone on the wooden balcony of Jeremy's apartment, his silk robe wrapped loosely round her naked and deeply satisfied body. He had said nothing more about Tim, but gently guided her hands, as he kissed her, teaching her how to give pleasure as well as receive it. A nightingale sang in a mango tree below, and the last of the raindrops sparkled like jewels on the fronds of the palm trees round the lawn. The sky was new washed, deep blue, and the moon and stars were luminous, matching her mood.

Gently a warm arm slid round her waist, and she turned to bury her face against his chest and press herself against the full length of him. She whispered, 'I thought you were asleep.'

'I missed you.' His lips were moving over her hair. Damp with perspiration, with the passionate exchanges of love, he gently stroked back strands of her hair, and kissed her cheek, her neck and throat. 'What were you thinking about all by yourself?'

Her voice was beginning to sound unsteady at the persistent attention of his mouth and tongue, the proximity of his warm flesh and the delightful inventiveness of his beloved hands. 'They were expecting us at the club about three hours ago. . .'

'Mmm, yes, darling. But what were you really thinking?'

'That I didn't think it was possible to be so happy.' The desires and longings that she had thought were appeased were beginning to be aroused yet again, and she turned to wrap her arms around his neck, holding him tightly against her. The silk robe fell to the ground, the moonlight glinting on its rich colours, and they left it where it fell as Jeremy picked her up in his arms and carried her back to his bed.

He said, looking down at her and touching her cheek gently, 'I think I knew you'd come when I called.'

'I never meant to come.'

He gave her that familiar, tantalising smile. 'Your heart meant to. It was your head that gave me a lot of trouble, my Ali.'

He moved alongside her on the satin sheets, took her into his embrace, lifting her to meet his lips, and there was no more need for talking.

MAY 1992 HARDBACK TITLES

——— ROMANCE ———

Law of the Circle *Rosalie Ash*	3684	0 263 13162 9
Feelings of Love *Anne Beaumont*	3685	0 263 13163 7
Stormfire *Helen Bianchin*	3686	0 263 13164 5
Stone Angel *Helen Brooks*	3687	0 263 13165 3
Last of the Great French Lovers *Sarah Holland*	3688	0 263 13166 1
Law of Attraction *Penny Jordan*	3689	0 263 13167 X
Cave of Fire *Rebecca King*	3690	0 263 13168 8
A Daring Proposition *Miranda Lee*	3691	0 263 13169 6
The Orchard King *Miriam Macgregor*	3692	0 263 13170 X
Dangerous Sanctuary *Anne Mather*	3693	0 263 13171 8
One Love Forever *Barbara McMahon*	3694	0 263 13172 6
Romantic Encounter *Betty Neels*	3695	0 263 13173 4
No Mistress but Love *Kate Proctor*	3696	0 263 13174 2
Intrigue *Margaret Mayo*	3697	0 263 13210 2
No Provocation *Sophie Weston*	3698	0 263 13176 9
Dark Forces *Sara Wood*	3699	0 263 13177 7

MASQUERADE *Historical*

Ten Guineas on Love *Alice Thornton*	M287	0 263 13261 7
The Golden Phoenix *Hazel Smith*	M288	0 263 13262 5

MEDICAL ROMANCE

The Call of Love *Jenny Ashe*	D205	0 263 13259 5
A Heart Untamed *Judith Worthy*	D206	0 263 13260 9

LARGE PRINT

Desperate Measures *Sara Craven*	519	0 263 13026 6
Mirror Image *Melinda Cross*	520	0 263 13027 4
Desert Destiny *Sarah Holland*	521	0 263 13028 2
Asking for Trouble *Miranda Lee*	522	0 263 13029 0
The Corsican Gambit *Sandra Marton*	523	0 263 13030 4
Fated Attraction *Carole Mortimer*	524	0 263 13031 2
A Kind of Magic *Betty Neels*	525	0 263 13032 0
Games for Sophisticates *Diana Hamilton*	526	0 263 13033 9

JUNE 1992 HARDBACK TITLES

——ROMANCE——

A Love to Last *Samantha Day*	3700	0 263 13204 8
The Trespasser *Jane Donnelly*	3701	0 263 13205 6
Revenge *Natalie Fox*	3702	0 263 13206 4
A Tempting Shore *Dana James*	3703	0 263 13207 2
Past Loving *Penny Jordan*	3704	0 263 13208 0
Yesterday and Forever *Sandra Marton*	3705	0 263 13209 9
Catalina's Lover *Vanessa Grant*	3706	0 263 13221 8
Second Chance for Love *Susanne McCarthy*	3707	0 263 13211 0
Winter of Dreams *Susan Napier*	3708	0 263 13212 9
The Final Surrender *Elizabeth Oldfield*	3709	0 263 13213 7
More than a Dream *Emma Richmond*	3710	0 263 13214 5
Old Love, New Love *Jennifer Taylor*	3711	0 263 13215 3
Knight to the Rescue *Miranda Lee*	3712	0 263 13216 1
No Gentleman *Kate Walker*	3713	0 263 13217 X
Out of Nowhere *Patricia Wilson*	3714	0 263 13218 8
Something in Return *Karen van der Zee*	3715	0 263 13219 6

MASQUERADE *Historical*

Heir Apparent *Petra Nash*	M289	0 263 13297 8
Scandal in the Sun *Yvonne Purves*	M290	0 263 13298 6

MEDICAL ROMANCE

Surgeon of the Heart *Sharon Wirdnam*	D207	0 263 13295 1
A Gentle Giant *Caroline Anderson*	D208	0 263 13296 X

LARGE PRINT

An Unusual Affair *Lindsay Armstrong*	527	0 263 13034 7
Summer Storms *Emma Goldrick*	528	0 263 13035 5
Past Passion *Penny Jordan*	529	0 263 13036 3
Forbidden Fruit *Charlotte Lamb*	530	0 263 13037 1
Weekend Wife *Sue Peters*	531	0 263 13038 X
Dear Miss Jones *Catherine Spencer*	532	0 263 13039 8
Bad Neighbours *Jessica Steele*	533	0 263 13040 1
Wild Streak *Kay Thorpe*	534	0 263 13041 X

LOOK OUT FOR OUR NEW MEDICAL LARGE PRINT SERIES. THESE ARE THE TITLES FOR APRIL – SEPTEMBER